the wizzle war

MACDONALD HALL

The Macdonald Hall Series

GORDON KORMAN

the wizzle war

MACDONALD HALL

Previous title:
The War with Mr. Wizzle

Cover photos by
Rodrigo Moreno and Luis Borba

Photo-illustration by
Yüksel Hassan

Scholastic Canada Ltd.
Toronto New York London Auckland Sydney
Mexico City New Delhi Hong Kong Buenos Aires

Scholastic Canada Ltd.
604 King Street West, Toronto, Ontario M5V 1E1, Canada

Scholastic Inc.
557 Broadway, New York, NY 10012, USA

Scholastic Australia Pty Limited
PO Box 579, Gosford, NSW 2250, Australia

Scholastic New Zealand Limited
Private Bag 94407, Greenmount, Auckland, New Zealand

Scholastic Children's Books
Euston House, 24 Eversholt Street, London NW1 1DB, UK

National Library of Canada Cataloguing in Publication

Korman, Gordon
[Bruno & Boots]
        The Wizzle war / Gordon Korman
(MacDonald Hall series)
Previously published as: Bruno & Boots : the war with Mr. Wizzle.
ISBN 0-439-96902-6
        I. Title. II. Series.
PS8571.O78T5 2003   jC813'.54   C2003-901314-6
PZ7

ISBN-10 0-439-96902-6 / ISBN-13 978-0-439-96902-4

6 5 4 3 2   Printed in Canada   08 09 10 11

For my friends in New York.
If we are the future,
can the world survive?

contents

Contents

Chapter 1

wizzleware

"He's not going to like it," Boots O'Neal said nervously to Wilbur Hackenschleimer and Larry Wilson. The three boys were draped in various poses over the furniture of room 306 in Dormitory 3.

"I don't like it much myself," grumbled big Wilbur. "The last time I wore a suit was at my aunt's wedding. The tie was so tight I couldn't even eat!"

"A dress code at Macdonald Hall!" exclaimed Larry in disgust. "Where did they get an idea like that anyway? There's never been a dress code at this school before!"

"All I know," repeated Boots with a sigh, "is that he's not going to like it. And when he gets here, who knows what he'll do?"

"*I* know what he'll do," said Wilbur sourly. "He'll rant and rave and tell us our world is crumbling around us."

"And," added Larry, "he'll holler about the sanctity of Macdonald Hall being threatened. And before you know it — "

"Bang!" finished Boots. "He'll have the whole campus organized and we'll be up to our ears in some crazy scheme!"

"Maybe he won't mind," suggested Larry hopefully. "I suppose there are worse things than having to wear a jacket and tie to classes."

"Name one," growled Wilbur.

"Well, there's . . . " Larry's voice trailed off. The sound of hurried footsteps in the corridor outside broke the silence. Boots flung open the door and in burst Sidney Rampulsky, stubbing his toe on the leg of the desk and flying full force into the wall. He picked himself up, grinned sheepishly and said, "Hi, guys. I thought I'd better warn you, Boots. The bus just got here, and he's on it."

Boots groaned.

"He's coming," said Wilbur sadly.

"How did he look?" asked Larry anxiously.

Sidney shrugged. "I don't know. Like he always looks."

Larry got up. "Maybe I'll go back to my room. I'm getting kind of nervous."

"Not me," said Wilbur. "I wouldn't miss this for the world!"

The four boys remained frozen as they heard footsteps coming down the hall. Then he was standing there in the doorway, his dark hair unruly as usual, a suitcase in each hand, a package under his arm, a wide grin showing his even white teeth.

Bruno Walton strolled into room 306, dropped his luggage unceremoniously on the floor and threw himself backward onto the bed that was traditionally his. He breathed deeply.

"Ah, Macdonald Hall air. It's great to be back!"

"Home sweet home," smiled Boots weakly. "Same old room."

"Same old faces," agreed Bruno, looking at the other boys. "Hi, Sidney — Wilbur — Larry. Good to see you." Without getting up, he extended his hand to Boots, his roommate and best friend. The two shook hands enthusiastically.

"He hasn't even mentioned it!" whispered Larry.

"So," said Boots heartily, "what kind of a summer did you have, Bruno?"

"Dull. That's why it's so good to be back at the Hall. Nothing ever happens at home."

"What is it that happens here?" asked Boots nervously.

Bruno shrugged. "You know — the usual. There's never a dull moment at Macdonald Hall. Hey, you've got to hear this! Something weird happened. When I got on the train, my mother handed me this package. She said it was a surprise and I shouldn't open it until I got to school. So I opened it on the train, and you won't believe what was in there! Two suits! Jackets, pants, shirts, ties! Has my mother gone nuts? I mean, what am I going to do with that stuff?"

Boots, Wilbur, Larry and Sidney exchanged uneasy glances.

Boots took a deep breath for courage. "Bruno, you're not going to like this, but here it is: There's a dress code at the Hall this year."

Bruno's jaw dropped. He stared at his roommate and mouthed the words, "Dress code?"

"Yeah," said Larry. "From now on, whenever we go out of our rooms, we have to wear a jacket and tie."

All the colour drained from Bruno's face. He sat in pained silence for a moment and then said, "Well, obviously there's been some mistake."

"No mistake," said Boots. "It's a new policy for Macdonald Hall."

Bruno looked thoughtful. "What a bummer!" He perked up and slapped Boots heartily on the shoulder. "Hey, don't worry about the dress code. We'll get rid of it in no time at all. Now, at dinner tonight, we'll get up a committee . . . "

* * *

William R. Sturgeon, Headmaster of Macdonald Hall, stood in the outer office and fixed the computer monitor with the cold gaze that, coupled with his surname, had earned him the nickname "The Fish" among his students. The computer stared back — or appeared to. The screen showed hundreds of thousands of lightning-fast operations — decades of student records being resorted and rearranged, a school's proud history converted to bundles of digital data. It was the Headmaster who looked away first.

"I find this difficult to accept," he said to his secretary, Mrs. Davis. "After so many years as part of a human institution, it's hard to believe that someone can download some new program and reduce our boys to a series of numbers."

"I can't get used to that Mr. Wizzle," said Mrs. Davis primly. "He and his software make me nervous. I can't help feeling that things are never going to be the same around here."

Mr. Sturgeon smiled sadly. "I suppose it's all in the name of progress."

"Progress!" repeated Mrs. Davis distastefully. "Just because a thing is new and modern doesn't make it good."

Into the office walked Walter C. Wizzle, a short, squat young man with jet-black, curly hair. He was impeccably dressed, and his step was jaunty, giving the impression of boundless energy.

"Good afternoon," he boomed. His voice had an enthusiasm that matched his walk. "I see you're admiring the new software. I wrote the code myself."

"I'm not sure admiration is the correct word, Wizzle," replied Mr. Sturgeon wryly.

"It makes the screen flicker," said Mrs. Davis coldly.

Mr. Wizzle smiled engagingly. "Oh, we'll all get used to that very soon," he promised.

"We *all* don't have to work beside it," replied Mrs. Davis pointedly.

Mr. Wizzle turned to the Headmaster. "Have you some time now, Mr. Sturgeon? I want to tell you about the PowerPoint presentation I've put together to show the students at tomorrow's assembly."

The two walked into the inner office and shut the door.

Mrs. Davis glared at the door and then at the computer.

"*Software!*" she muttered. "Soft in the head would be more like it!"

Mr. Wizzle settled back comfortably in the visitor's chair. "Now, I propose to explain to the students exactly what WizzleWare is for — to modernize an out-of-date school."

Mr. Sturgeon's knuckles whitened on the arm of his chair. "May I remind you that this out-of-date school has the highest academic standing in all of Ontario!"

"Admittedly," said Mr. Wizzle. "But everything is so hopelessly old-fashioned. The teaching methods are from a bygone era. The systems are archaic. WizzleWare and I going to change all that."

"Then what," asked Mr. Sturgeon, "is the purpose of your dress code? I should think modernization would go with a more relaxed atmosphere."

"I explained that to Mr. Snow and your Board of Directors when they hired me. My theory of handling students is based on my own recent psychological research. Modern education is open enough, but too permissive. My new system retains the openness but adds discipline. The theory is that a boy who is sloppily dressed will slouch, and the sloppiness will extend to his work. A boy who is smartly dressed will sit up straight, be more alert and turn out better work."

The Headmaster nodded slowly. "And the Board of Directors agreed with you?"

"Better than that," said Mr. Wizzle enthusiastically. "They voted unanimously to give me a free hand to transform Macdonald Hall into the school of the future!"

Mr. Sturgeon nodded again, but his expression clearly stated his fondness for the school of the past.

The young man seemed to sense this. "With, of course, some input from you as Headmaster."

"Naturally," said Mr. Sturgeon grimly.

* * *

At a corner table in the dining hall, Bruno Walton was holding a council of war.

"All right, you guys, who knows anything about this dress code?"

"Well," began studious Elmer Drimsdale, "starting tomorrow morning with the opening assembly, everyone must wear a jacket and tie for all school functions, including classes and meals — "

"Yeah, yeah, we all know *that*," said Bruno impatiently. "What I want to know is why The Fish would do this to us! We've never had a dress code here before. And it's not as though any of us ever go around dressed in real rags. What's going on?"

"I don't know if this has anything to do with it," put in Larry Wilson, who was Mr. Sturgeon's office messenger, "but I checked in at the office half an hour ago and it's, like, nuts. Every computer in the place is running some crazy new software program, and half of them are down because they don't have enough memory!"

"Software?"

"Yes," said Elmer, his eyes lighting up behind his thick glasses. "While I don't recognize the program itself, it is clearly an example of a new generation of software. It makes use of superior processing speed and algorithmic multi-tasking to simulate real brain function. Now more than ever, computers can *think*."

"No, that can't be it," said Bruno with characteristic

single-mindedness. "Computers don't care what we wear. Haven't you guys heard anything at all about the dress code?"

"Maybe they'll explain it at the assembly tomorrow morning," suggested Mark Davies, the editor of the school newspaper.

"But we'll be in our ties by then!" protested Bruno. "I want to knock this thing off before it gets started!"

"I don't understand what all the fuss is about," said Elmer, who habitually sported a white shirt and neat black tie. "There's nothing wrong with wearing a tie."

"It's uncomfortable," complained Chris Talbot.

"And you can't eat," added Wilbur, lifting his head out of the huge casserole he was tackling.

"I can't *move* in a tie!" put in Sidney Rampulsky.

"That's good," grinned Boots. "That's a plus. If Sidney can't move, he won't be falling down and breaking things."

"Aw, lay off!" Sidney gestured in annoyance and accidentally thrust his hand into the hot mashed potatoes. "Ow!"

A roar of laughter rocked the dining hall.

Bruno stood up and pounded the table. "How can you laugh when our world is crumbling around us? The sanctity of Macdonald Hall is being threatened! You guys don't seem to realize the seriousness of this situation! Tomorrow morning you'll have to put your necks in a noose! Now, as chairman of the Anti-Dress-Code Committee, I'm going to lead the delegation to The Fish's house tonight. Who's coming with me?"

There was dead silence, broken only by the sound of Wilbur slurping at his dinner.

"Come on!" groaned Bruno, annoyed. "You can't expect Boots and me to go alone!"

"Me? Why me?" squealed Boots. "I didn't volunteer for anything!"

"You're vice-chairman of the committee," explained Bruno. "You have to go. Come on, I need some volunteers. Wilbur, Elmer, Sidney, Chris, Larry, Mark — there, that's enough. That should do it."

"I don't want to go," said Sidney plaintively.

"It's all arranged," said Bruno. "We'll go right after dinner and settle this once and for all."

* * *

"Mildred," said Mr. Sturgeon to his wife, "Walter C. Wizzle is an idiot."

Mrs. Sturgeon poured the after-dinner coffee. "Now, dear," she said soothingly, "you haven't given the young man a chance."

"I've known him for over a month and my opinion stands," said the Headmaster sourly. "Besides, he doesn't need a chance from me. He has WizzleWare *and* the Board of Directors on his side."

"WizzleWare?"

"His software program. He wrote it just for Macdonald Hall. How fortunate for us!" He stirred his coffee violently. "Do you know what he had the nerve to tell me right to my face? He called our school out-of-date! And hopelessly old-fashioned! And archaic! What do you think of that, Mildred?"

"You have to make allowances for his enthusiasm. After all, he's just out of university and eager to try out his new ideas."

"Why does he have to try them on my school?" complained the Headmaster. "Why don't things like Wizzle-Ware happen to other schools?"

The doorbell rang.

"I'll get it," said Mr. Sturgeon wearily. "Maybe it's Wizzle with another PowerPoint presentation. I wish I had the power to point him straight out the main gate . . . " He opened the door to reveal Bruno, Boots and the rest of the committee.

"Hello, sir." Bruno greeted him with genuine pleasure. "How was your summer?"

"Very busy and very enjoyable, thank you," said the Headmaster briskly. "It's good to see you back again, Walton — O'Neal — boys." He acknowledged them all with a curt nod. "Is there something I can do for you?"

"Well, sir," said Bruno, "as a matter of fact, we've been doing a lot of talking about the new dress code."

"Oh?" said the Headmaster noncommitally.

"Yes, sir. We were wondering, since there's never been one before — uh — we discussed — and, uh — well, sir, how about calling it off?"

A smile tugged at Mr. Sturgeon's thin lips, but he stifled the impulse. "You'll be told all about everything tomorrow at the assembly."

"But, sir, tomorrow the dress code will already have started!" Bruno blurted in dismay.

"Yes," agreed Mr. Sturgeon. "And please abide by it. I'll see you all tomorrow in the auditorium. Good evening." He shut the door on the committee and returned to the dining room.

"Who was at the door, William?"

The Headmaster sat down, chuckling with great satisfaction. "I think, Mildred, that it was the thorn in Wizzle's paw."

She frowned. "What on earth are you talking about?"

"It was Walton and O'Neal and a delegation of boys come to tell me they don't like the dress code." He laughed. "I'll bet WizzleWare doesn't have a category for Walton."

"Are you hoping for trouble for poor Mr. Wizzle?" she accused.

He looked at her righteously. "Archaic indeed!"

* * *

"Bruno, go to sleep!" exclaimed Boots O'Neal from the bed near the window.

"Never!" growled Bruno. "If I go to sleep, I'll have to wake up; and when I wake up, I'll have to put on a tie!" He tossed violently, kicking at his blanket. "Did you hear what The Fish said? 'Obey the dress code!' Just like that!"

"If you don't go to sleep," explained Boots patiently, "morning will probably come anyway. Either way, you're wearing a tie."

"A petition!" raved Bruno. "We'll get up a petition!"

"Bruno . . . " yawned Boots.

"And demonstrations!" added Bruno, warming to the subject. "We'll organize lots of protest demonstrations! And we'll burn a whole stack of ties in front of the Faculty Building!"

"Right," agreed Boots indulgently. "First thing in the morning. Now go to sleep."

"The girls will help us," Bruno went on enthusiastically. "We'll have to sneak across to Scrimmage's tomorrow night."

Boots put his head under the pillow and groaned. The thought of involving the girls from Miss Scrimmage's Finishing School for Young Ladies, located across the highway from Macdonald Hall, alarmed him. Some of the girls were wildly unpredictable.

"Yeah, that's it," concluded Bruno triumphantly. "We'll call in Cathy and Diane and the troops. That dress code is as good as gone!" He rolled over and promptly went to sleep.

Boots tossed and turned, sleepless.

Chapter 2

dressed to kill

"I can't breathe!" gasped Bruno Walton, standing stiff as a board and staring wild-eyed into the mirror.

"It's awful," agreed Boots in a strained voice. He craned his neck gingerly and peered over Bruno's shoulder into the mirror. "Look at us. We look like accountants! How can we be expected to eat breakfast in these outfits?"

"How can we be expected to eat breakfast, *period*?" howled Bruno. It had always been his custom to sleep until quarter to nine, missing breakfast altogether, and then to make a frantic effort to get to his first class more or less on time. Now the necessity of being nattily dressed was forcing him to get up earlier. "I can't stand it!"

The scene was similar in every room in Macdonald Hall.

"This tie doesn't look nice and neat like yours," complained Wilbur Hackenschleimer to his roommate, Larry Wilson. "And I can't get it to hang right."

"Well, that's because you haven't done up the top button of your shirt," said Larry.

Wilbur staggered backward. "You mean you have to do up the top button?"

"Of course."

"You mean the *top* button? The one at the very *top*? Right where your *neck* is?" gasped Wilbur.

"Yes."

Wilbur turned and looked at his sad, forlorn face in the mirror. "Here goes . . . "

"What's the matter with you?" Chris Talbot shouted at his roommate, Pete Anderson. "You can't wear a yellow-and-black striped shirt with a purple tie!"

"All right," said Pete. "I'll take the tie off. What goes with a yellow-and-black striped shirt?"

"Pollen," said Chris in disgust. "You look like a *bee*."

"How do you tie this thing?" asked Sidney Rampulsky, standing in confusion in the middle of the room.

"Leave me alone!" growled Mark Davies. "I'm miserable enough!"

"Now, let's see . . . " said Sidney. "I guess you loop these together and pull the end through here. Does that look all right?"

"Gorgeous!" muttered Mark without looking up. "Let's go."

They started for the door, but Sidney stopped abruptly. "Hey, my tie's caught on something." He grabbed the tie and pulled. With an odd crunching noise, the hanging

16

light fixture was ripped from the ceiling and came crashing down on Sidney's head. Sidney went sprawling onto the desk, dazed.

"Oh, you klutz!"

In the dining hall the atmosphere was positively pained. Most of the boys sat in silent, stiff-necked misery.

"This looks like the International Zombie Convention," remarked Bruno savagely. "It just isn't Macdonald Hall anymore."

"Hey, Bruno," called Larry, adding insult to injury. "White shirt, red tie — you look like your throat's been cut."

"At least my tie doesn't have a big green palm tree on it," retorted Bruno. "Yours would go best with a grass skirt."

"Get out of here with those polka dots! I'm trying to eat!"

"You know, the thick end is supposed to hang lower than the thin end. But I suppose that doesn't apply to silver ties."

"I can't breathe!"

"Hey, stupid, your jacket's inside out!"

"A silver tie? *Where*?"

"Everything tastes the same."

"Perry's tie has a sunburst on it."

"Perry's tie has scrambled egg on it!"

"Help!"

Mark Davies appeared, leading Sidney by the arm. "Get Sidney some food," he ordered briskly. "He had a little accident this morning."

"What happened?" asked Bruno.

"His tie got caught in the light fixture and he pulled half the ceiling down on his head," explained Mark. He grabbed one of the rolls from Wilbur's plate. "Here, Sidney, eat."

Sidney ate.

"He's the first casualty of the dress code," declared Bruno decisively.

Elmer Drimsdale rushed over with a glass of chocolate milk. "Here, Sidney, drink."

Sidney drank.

"It will be good for him," Elmer explained as Sidney mindlessly drained the glass. "There is a mild stimulant in chocolate."

"Do you think he's okay?" asked Boots anxiously.

"Hey," exclaimed Larry, "five minutes to assembly! We'd better get going!"

* * *

"Good morning, boys," said Mr. Sturgeon, standing up at the podium to address the assembled student body. "Welcome to Macdonald Hall and, in most cases, welcome back. For those of you who are new here, I am Mr. Sturgeon, your headmaster." He paused to clear his throat carefully. "This is going to be a — special year at Macdonald Hall. There will be some changes made. Doubtless you have noticed a few already, for instance, the dress code which we have not had before.

"I would now like to introduce to you the gentleman who is in charge of these changes. It is his responsibility to examine and evaluate our systems and to alter them where he deems necessary. Mr. Walter C. Wizzle."

There was a bit of dutiful applause, but it was thinly scattered throughout the auditorium. Most of the boys had already put two and two together and blamed Mr.

Wizzle for the dress code and their present discomfort.

Mr. Wizzle made his bouncing way up to the microphone. "Good morning, gentlemen," he greeted the boys. "I must say that you're a very smart-looking lot. I'm sure this is an improvement on previous opening assemblies."

There was a murmur from the crowd which Mr. Wizzle didn't seem to notice and which the Headmaster quelled with one cold look. Mr. Wizzle cleared his throat and launched into the speech he had prepared.

"We live in a rapidly changing world," he began, "a world where advanced technology creates limitless possibilities . . . "

"Uh-oh," whispered Bruno to Boots in the fifth row. "It's going to be one of those Let's-meet-the-challenge-of-the-future speeches."

Mr. Wizzle was warming to his subject. "As an outstanding academic institution, Macdonald Hall must keep pace with these changes. And as the citizens of tomorrow, its students must be prepared to meet the challenges of the future."

Bruno nudged Boots. "What did I tell you?"

"Shhh!" whispered Boots nervously.

"I will be spending a lot of time with all of you," Mr. Wizzle continued briskly, "helping you meet these challenges. I will be attending your classes, making changes in some of them and organizing others; I will be planning new extracurricular activities; I will be making reports and recommendations at staff and administration meetings, and I will oversee their implementation. In short, I will be working with all of you to make Macdonald Hall a better place."

"I like it just the way it is!" fumed Bruno.

"*Shhh!*" whispered Boots. "The Fish is looking at *us!*"

"In this new millennium, any school that doesn't keep pace — including Macdonald Hall — is in danger of becoming a dinosaur. And you all know," said Mr. Wizzle, smiling at his own joke, "what happened to the dinosaurs."

Bruno's face was turning a deep beet-red.

"We must ensure that Macdonald Hall doesn't suffer the same fate, or you young men will ultimately be the losers."

Bruno squirmed in his chair.

"Right now this school is simply out of date."

Flaming with fury, Bruno leapt to his feet and opened his mouth to yell, but two hands clamped over his mouth just in time. Boots and Wilbur, flanking Bruno, gently but firmly eased him back into his seat.

"Now," Mr. Wizzle said, "here are the changes that I have already implemented. There is the dress code, to which there will be no exceptions. There is a system of demerit points for all breaking of rules: Anyone accumulating ten demerit points will see me in my office, and I will assign the appropriate punishment. Demerits can be assigned by any member of the teaching staff. There will be frequent dormitory inspections, so we expect a lot of spit and polish in the rooms, hmmm?"

Mr. Wizzle paused and beamed at them. "You are probably asking yourselves how I can do all this work. Well, I have a special assistant. It's called WizzleWare — the most advanced educational and administrative software program in the world today. Join with us as we bring

Macdonald Hall into the vanguard of Canadian private schools." He stopped for applause. There was none.

"That is, of course, not without some feedback from you students," Wizzle continued. "There will be a suggestion box in the front hall of each dormitory. I welcome your suggestions on how we can all make Macdonald Hall a better place."

"I know how we can make Macdonald Hall a better place!" growled Bruno under his breath. "Kick *him* out!"

Mr. Wizzle pointed to Bruno. "You in the fifth row — yes, you with the red tie. What's your name?"

Bruno stood up. "Walton, sir. Bruno Walton."

From his jacket pocket Mr. Wizzle produced a note pad and pencil. "Bruno Walton," he said scribbling on the pad. "Five demerits for unseemly conduct during assembly." He gazed out over the crowd. "That will be all. You are dismissed."

No one moved.

Mr. Sturgeon stood up. "You may go," he said quietly.

The boys began to file out of the auditorium. Sidney Rampulsky got to his feet. An odd look came over his face and he announced loudly, "I don't feel very well." He tottered a few steps and then keeled over, out cold. An entire row of chairs went down with him.

"It's his tie!" bellowed Bruno, pushing his way toward the fallen Sidney. "Loosen his tie! Stand back! Give him air!" He shoved at someone in a grey pinstripe suit.

"Kindly stop pushing, Walton," said the cold voice of Mr. Sturgeon, who had rushed from the platform to Sidney's aid.

Sidney's eyelids fluttered open, and he looked up, smiling sweetly. "Oh, Mr. Sturgeon, I had a little accident this morning."

The Headmaster sighed. "I've told you to be more careful with yourself, Rampulsky. What happened to you this time?"

"It was all because of the dress code, sir," piped Bruno. "He was — "

"Thank you, Walton. Rampulsky is capable of speech."

"I was tying my tie," explained Sidney weakly, "when suddenly the fixture came down on my head."

"See?" said Bruno triumphantly. "The dress code!"

"Bruno Walton," called the voice of Mr. Wizzle. "Your remarks and interruptions are uncalled-for. That will be another two demerits."

Mr. Sturgeon suppressed a strange smile. "Come along, Rampulsky," he said, helping Sidney to his feet. "I think perhaps you'd better spend some time in the infirmary."

* * *

"Bruno, will you calm down!" exclaimed Boots in exasperation.

"Walter C. Wizzle!" steamed Bruno in disgust. "The demerit system!"

"You're only upset about that because you got slapped with the first ones," argued Boots.

"Your turn will come," Bruno snarled. "He's out to get all of us!" He ripped off his tie and threw himself backward onto his bed. "He called Macdonald Hall out of date — 'in danger of becoming a dinosaur!' Well, let me tell you right now that *this* dinosaur is going to stomp all over his face!"

Boots sat down heavily at his desk. "What can we do

about it? He was hired by the school, probably by the Board of Directors."

"Well, we sure can't let him ruin the Hall like this!" exclaimed Bruno. "Where's that suggestion box? *I* have a suggestion!"

"You'll only get more demerits for that kind of suggestion," warned Boots.

"I don't intend to sign it," said Bruno. "Anyway, it's all decided. Wizzle must go!"

"How?"

Bruno shrugged. "The Anti-Dress-Code Committee changes its name to the Anti-Wizzle Committee." He squared his jaw. "That's the way things are done. You identify the enemy, and then you fight!"

"Let's go visit Sidney in the infirmary," suggested Boots, trying to change the subject.

"Good idea," said Bruno. "We can tell him all about the new committee."

"Bruno, he has a concussion. He doesn't need to hear about the new committee."

"Let's go."

The two boys walked out into the hall of Dormitory 3 to find Walter C. Wizzle himself, equipped with hammer and nails, affixing a large box to the wall just inside the front door.

Mr. Wizzle glared. "Bruno Walton again. Aren't you forgetting something, young man?"

"Sir?"

"Your tie," said Mr. Wizzle sternly. "Violation of the dress code is quite a serious offence. However, since it is the first day, and you haven't actually left the building, I will assign you only one demerit." He made a note on his pad.

Bruno rushed back and put on his tie. When he returned, Mr. Wizzle had gone and Boots was staring at the box. It was the size of a breadbox, with a padlock holding down the lid, and a slit near the top. On it was stencilled: FEEDBACK BOX.

Bruno reached for the pad and pencil which sat on a shelf below the box. He stared. At the top of each page of the pad was printed the word *Feedback*.

"Feedback!" said Bruno in disgust. "That must be a Wizzle word!" On the paper he wrote: MACDONALD HALL LIVES in block letters. "How's that for *feedback?*"

"Fine," sighed Boots.

* * *

Mr. Sturgeon was on the telephone with Mr. James Snow, Chairman of the Macdonald Hall Board of Directors.

"Jim, about this man Wizzle. His methods seem so — unusual. Have you checked into his background? . . . Oh, I'm sure you and the Board have good reason to think that he's a genius, but sometimes theory doesn't apply well in practice . . . Well, classes haven't even started yet, and already I can feel the tension on this campus . . . Quite frankly, I thought my boys were going to lynch him after he spoke at the assembly this morning . . . Yes, perhaps it does prove that the boys need more discipline, but . . . Very well, Jim. I don't want it said of me that I don't give a man a chance. Good day."

The Headmaster hung up and turned to his wife. "Mildred, I've come to the conclusion that Jim Snow knows as much about education as Wizzle does."

"William, I think Mr. Snow is right," said Mrs. Sturgeon.

"You really have condemned poor Mr. Wizzle before allowing him to get started."

"Oh, he got started," said the Headmaster, grim humour tempering his anger. "He started today. He introduced the demerit system and Walton got seven at the assembly alone. At this rate, the boy will have hundreds by Christmas."

"I don't find that very funny," said his wife severely.

"You weren't there, Mildred. O'Neal and Hackenschleimer had to hold Walton down to keep him from rushing the podium. I believe that was when Wizzle called Macdonald Hall 'simply out of date.'"

"Oh dear," said Mrs. Sturgeon. "I don't like the sound of that."

Mr. Sturgeon laughed mirthlessly. "Neither did Walton. You know, we'll have to watch this situation very carefully, Mildred, or we could have a full-scale revolution on our hands."

* * *

"Come on," prompted Bruno. "It's past midnight. Just over the sill and across the road like always."

"I don't want to go to Scrimmage's tonight," said Boots nervously. "If we get caught, we'll both get demerits."

"I never get caught," scoffed Bruno. "And I don't intend to start now."

"For a guy who already has eight demerits," Boots pointed out, "you have a lot of confidence."

"Come on. Let's go."

With Bruno in the lead, the two boys eased themselves out the window of room 306, scampered silently over the campus and across the highway, and scaled the wrought-iron fence surrounding Miss Scrimmage's Finishing School for Young Ladies. Bruno tossed a handful of pebbles at a second-storey window.

A face appeared at the window and an arm beckoned. Bruno and Boots shinnied up the drainpipe and were helped over the sill and into the room.

"Hi," said dark-haired Cathy Burton with a broad smile. "Welcome once again to our humble abode."

"How are you guys?" asked blonde Diane Grant, Cathy's roommate. "Did you have a good summer?"

"It was an okay summer," said Bruno. "It's the fall, winter and spring that worry me."

"Bruno's on the campaign trail again," explained Boots.

"I don't even want to hear about it!" exclaimed Cathy. "We've got troubles of our own over here!"

"What's wrong?" asked Bruno, mystified. Cathy was always the first one to jump at the chance to become involved in other people's problems. What kind of trouble could have dampened her enthusiasm?

"We're worried about Miss Scrimmage," said Cathy. "She's been acting old and decrepit."

"But she *is* old and decrepit," put in Boots.

"Of course she is," said Cathy impatiently. "But this year suddenly she's talking about some big changes at the school here. I've tried to pump her for information but all she says is, 'You'll find out soon enough.' Today she said, 'There'll be a big surprise for you tomorrow,' and not another word. You know how it drives me crazy when I'm not on top of the situation. What could Miss Scrimmage be up to?"

"It doesn't matter," said Bruno, making himself comfortable on a scatter rug. "You'll find out tomorrow. *We* found out today. It's big trouble — Macdonald Hall has hired this guy to change the school. Walter C. Wizzle. The 'C' is for computer — he wrote a software program to mess up our lives. You won't believe this, but they've stuck us with a dress code! And we're on a demerit system! He's giving everybody demerits!"

"Not everybody," corrected Boots. "Just you."

"Your turn will come," promised Bruno. "Anyway, that's the situation. We need your advice on how to get rid of this guy."

"Surely The Fish won't let him ruin Macdonald Hall," said Cathy. "It means too much to his cold, fishy heart."

"The Fish is going along with Wizzle," said Bruno. "I don't understand it. It's as though he wants all this."

"It doesn't sound so bad to me," said Diane timidly. "There's nothing wrong with new technology."

"Not while I'm strangling in a tie," said Bruno shortly, "and piling up a stack of demerits that you can't see over. And sitting in a Wizzle class. Who knows what a guy like that will decide we should learn?"

"Sounds pretty grim," agreed Cathy.

"It is," replied Boots. "And it looks as if it's going to get worse."

"What can we do to help?" asked Diane warily.

Bruno grinned broadly. "We came to you for feedback."

"*Feedback?*"

"A Wizzle word," he explained. "It means suggestions and stuff." His dark eyes looked into Cathy's blue ones. "We've got to get rid of this guy! Unless you want to see us turned into a bunch of robots with ties in a fifth-rate school, you've got to help us do something!"

"We'll give you as much help as you want," said Cathy immediately.

"We will?" asked Diane, her heart sinking.

"Of course. We can't let Macdonald Hall go to pot. Besides, it could be fun." Cathy's eyes sparkled. "What do you want us to do?"

"Well," said Bruno thoughtfully, "so far, the only thing we've come up with is anonymous suggestions in the Feedback boxes Wizzle's hung up in the dorms. Stuff like 'Macdonald Hall Lives.' If everybody writes them, maybe he'll get the message."

"Good," Cathy nodded. "Very good. What about an underground newspaper?"

Light dawned on Bruno's face. "Of course! *The Macdonald Hall Free Press!* We can all write articles for it! We'll start first thing in the morning!"

Boots frowned. "You know, we have The Fish to think about, too. He may not like changes at the Hall very much, but he's still not going to let us revolt."

"A newspaper isn't a revolt," insisted Bruno. "It's part of the democratic process — freedom of the press. When Wizzle and The Fish and the Board see our opinions honestly and tastefully expressed, they'll have to pay attention."

"But, Bruno — "

"It's settled, and as coeditor, you should be very proud!"

"Let's go home," mumbled Boots dejectedly. "It's getting late."

"Yeah," agreed Bruno. "Thanks a lot for the idea, girls. If we need any more help, we'll be back."

"Any time," said Cathy cheerfully. "Meanwhile, keep your fingers crossed that Miss Scrimmage's surprise isn't anything horrible. Good night."

The two boys shinnied down the drainpipe and retraced their steps to their own room. They climbed in and shut the window behind them.

"What a crummy year this is starting out to be," complained Boots. "Problems at the Hall, maybe problems at Scrimmage's."

"Don't worry," said Bruno. "Everything will be back to normal in no time."

There was a sharp rap on the door. "What's going on in there?" came the voice of Walter C. Wizzle. "It's one AM. Why are you boys still up?"

"We're just going to sleep," called Bruno as he and Boots dove fully dressed into their beds and pulled the blankets up to their necks.

There was the sound of a key turning in the lock, and Mr. Wizzle walked into the room, switching on the overhead light as he entered.

"Bruno Walton again. And who is your roommate?"

"Boots — I mean, Melvin O'Neal, sir," said Boots in a small voice.

Mr. Wizzle made a note on his pad. "Five demerits for each of you. Don't violate curfew again." He studied the pad. "Hmmm — Walton, you have thirteen demerits. I'll see you in my office tomorrow morning at precisely eight o'clock."

He switched off the light and left the room.

"Walter C. Wizzle!" muttered Bruno.

Chapter 3

balloonjuice!

"Is Mr. Wizzle in?" asked Bruno halfheartedly. It was eight o'clock the following morning, and he was reporting to account for the first ten of his thirteen demerits.

Mrs. Davis's pleasant smile faded abruptly. "Oh, Bruno, classes haven't even started yet! Don't tell me you're in trouble already!"

"I got some demerits," grinned Bruno sheepishly. He stretched his neck in a vain effort to escape the viselike grip of his tie. "Hey, Mrs. Davis, is that the new program?" He pointed to the computer, which was sorting files in a blizzard of on-screen data.

The secretary sighed. "That's it. WizzleWare."

Mr. Wizzle bounced enthusiastically into the office.

"Good morning, Mrs. Davis. Ah, Bruno Walton. Come into my office for a moment."

Bruno followed Mr. Wizzle into a small room off the reception area. "But, *sir*," he said in surprise, "isn't this Mr. Flynn's office?"

"Mr. Flynn is a phys. ed. teacher," said Mr. Wizzle. "His office is now in the gymnasium. Okay, Walton, you've managed to get more than ten demerits by various infractions of the rules. By tomorrow morning I want to see two hundred lines of 'I will obey fully all the rules of Macdonald Hall.'"

Bruno's jaw dropped. "*Lines,* sir?"

"Yes, lines," said Mr. Wizzle. "You may go now."

Bruno walked out of the office and came face to face with Mr. Sturgeon, who was talking to his secretary.

"Good morning, sir."

"Good morning, Walton. Mrs. Davis tells me that Mr. Wizzle has had to punish you."

"Yes, sir," replied Bruno, studying the carpet. "And I'd better get going. I've got two hundred lines to finish for tomorrow. Mr. Wizzle sure is riding the wave of the future." He blinked innocently.

"That will do, Walton." Mr. Sturgeon fixed him with a cold, fishy glare. "On your way."

Bruno scampered off down the hall and the Headmaster strolled into Mr. Wizzle's office.

"Lines, Wizzle? *Lines?*"

Mr. Wizzle looked up from his desk brightly. "Certainly. A young mind is always active and expanding. To be forced to write lines limits the opportunities for psychic growth. Therefore, it is all the more potent as punishment."

"I see." The Headmaster nodded. "Bore them to tears, is that it?"

"Essentially, yes," replied Mr. Wizzle earnestly. "Oh, by the way, Mr. Sturgeon, I've arranged a staff meeting for four o'clock Thursday."

"Have you?" said Mr. Sturgeon coldly.

"Yes. Tomorrow morning in period one I'm holding psychological tests for all students. With WizzleWare, I should have the results fully analyzed by Thursday afternoon."

"It should be interesting," said the Headmaster with a thin smile.

* * *

"He gives lines?" asked Boots incredulously at the breakfast table.

"Nobody gives lines anymore," said Mark Davies positively.

"He does," said Bruno. "But forget the lines. Here's how we're going to get rid of Wizzle. We're going to put out an underground newspaper and fight for our rights."

"That's a great idea!" said Chris.

"That's a terrible idea!" exclaimed Mark. "The minute it appears they'll know it came from the print shop and I'll be in trouble!"

"No you won't," said Bruno. "You'll teach Boots and me how to run the printing press, and when Wizzle or The Fish asks you if you did it, you can truthfully say no."

"Aw, Bruno — " protested Mark.

"Don't worry," said Bruno. "It's foolproof. Good idea, right, guys?"

"We'll all be expelled," said Wilbur mournfully between bites.

"They'll never catch us," said Bruno confidently.

"Now, all you guys spread the word around the school. We want articles and things from everybody against the dress code and against changing Macdonald Hall." He grinned. "We'll need lots of *feedback*."

Boots groaned. "I hate that word."

"Feedback is a very useful term," said Elmer earnestly. "It refers to the return of the output of a system to the input."

Bruno looked at him suspiciously. "I have absolutely no idea what you just said. But it had better not mean you're a Wizzle supporter."

"No," said Elmer. "I don't think Mr. Wizzle is good for Macdonald Hall."

"Right," said Bruno, "and that's the theme of your article for our newspaper *The Macdonald Hall Free Press*. As editor, I'm assigning the deadline — tonight."

"We have to get ready for classes tomorrow," Mark pointed out.

"Naturally we won't let that get in our way," said Bruno.

"You haven't got time to be a big-shot editor," said Boots. "You've got two hundred lines to write."

"Oh," said Bruno airily, "I've already thought of that. Poor Sidney is stuck in the infirmary, dying of boredom. He'll write my lines for me."

"Sidney will just love that!" said Boots sarcastically.

"Well, he's bound to see the logic," replied Bruno. "It helps him pass the time, and it leaves me free to work on the newspaper for the good of us all."

Mark looked at Bruno warningly. "If you wreck my printing press . . . "

"Mildred," said Mr. Sturgeon, entering the house at lunchtime, "if I were to tell you that someone at this school was giving lines for punishment, who would you say it might be?"

"Oh, William, not Mr. Wizzle!"

"Bull's eye," said the Headmaster, sitting down at the dining room table. "Have you ever heard of such a thing? Look who's calling Macdonald Hall a dinosaur! Lines! This is the most idiotic, outmoded — "

"Now, dear," said his wife soothingly, "I'm sure Mr. Wizzle must have a good reason."

"Oh, he certainly does," said the Headmaster, savagely attacking a stuffed tomato. "It was a bunch of gibberish about young minds and psychic growth, and it meant about as much as everything else he says — nothing. And do you know what he's done? He's called a staff meeting without consulting me!" He dropped his knife and fork with a clatter. "Mildred, how are we to get rid of him?"

"Dear, you're getting all excited about nothing," said Mrs. Sturgeon. "Classes haven't even started yet and you've already condemned Mr. Wizzle. Be fair, and I'm sure everything will turn out all right."

* * *

Miss Scrimmage's girls were assembled in the school gym, awaiting the announcement of the Headmistress's promised surprise.

"Lately I've been noticing I'm not as young as I used to be," she was saying. "There is a great deal of work at a school like this, and our Regents have been kind enough

34

to hire an administrative assistant to help me run it."

In the seventh row Diane nudged Cathy. "Oh, no! We're getting a Wizzle, too!"

"Don't worry," Cathy whispered confidently. "Miss Scrimmage probably picked some sweet old thing who's even more of a pushover than she is."

"We're very fortunate to get Miss Peabody, who has vast experience with young ladies," the Headmistress went on. "She comes to us from Fort Constitution near Seattle, Washington, which, as you may know, is a Marine training centre. Young ladies, I'd like to introduce you to Miss Peabody."

Scattered applause broke the shocked silence. Onto the podium marched former drill sergeant, now assistant Headmistress, Gloria Peabody. She was a tall, trim young woman dressed in a severe pantsuit. Her hair was pulled back and tied in a tight bun. Black high-heeled shoes with metal reinforcements at toe and heel clicked loudly with every step. She walked up to the microphone and surveyed the girls sternly.

"Good afternoon. I'm very pleased to be at such a fine institution as Miss Scrimmage's Finishing School for Young Ladies."

Cathy poked Diane and snickered loudly.

Miss Peabody pounced on her like a hawk. "All right, you! On your feet!"

Cathy stood up slowly. "Me?"

"Of course, you! Now get up here! March!"

Cathy walked to the front of the group.

"Straighten that back!" Miss Peabody leaned forward until her face was only a few centimetres away from

Cathy's and stared the girl right in the eye. "Name!" she barked.

"Cathy Burton, Ma'am."

"Burton, you'd better know right now that we do not tolerate any insolence in this outfit!"

"But, Miss Peabody," said Cathy innocently, "I have this terrible allergy and I was simply clearing my throat and —"

"Attention!" bellowed Miss Peabody.

Everybody jumped. Involuntarily, Cathy straightened her back and slapped her arms to her sides.

"All right, Burton, that'll cost you five laps around the track."

"But it's an 800-metre track!" blurted Cathy in protest.

"Six laps!" snapped Miss Peabody. "Right after afternoon classes."

"Yes, Miss Peabody," said Cathy, who had no intention of running any laps at all.

Miss Peabody read her mind. "And don't think you're going to get away with anything. I'm going to watch you and make sure you run every inch. Okay, sit down!"

As Cathy fled back to her seat, Miss Peabody surveyed the girls again. She smiled kindly. "We are all going to have a wonderful year here at Miss Scrimmage's."

And that's an order! thought Cathy bitterly.

* * *

"Okay." Bruno sat cross-legged on his bed, a sheaf of papers in his hand. "Here are the articles for the *Free Press*. Let's see what we've got." He handed half the papers to Boots.

The two boys read in silence for a few minutes.

"These are really lousy!" said Bruno. "Listen to this: *I think Macdonald Hall was a swell school until Mr. Wizzle came along and ruined it. Now everyone has to wear a tie and it's no good and awful.* What kind of journalism is that?"

"Better than this." Boots laughed. "*I hate Mr. Wizzle because he is dumb and stupid and makes you wear ties.* Or this one: *If a certain somebody doesn't stop calling Macdonald Hall a dinosaur and go elsewhere immediately, he will be fed to his software program post-haste!*"

"That one's great," approved Bruno. "We'll use it."

"Bruno, freedom of the press doesn't extend to threats."

"How about this?" suggested Bruno. "*Wearing a tie and a stiff shirt impedes the most important kind of processing of all, the intake of food, and thus is conducive to starvation. So let's all come to our senses and think back to how great things used to be when we could eat properly.* Guess who?"

Boots was hysterical with laughter. "We can't print that! Everyone in the world would know it's Wilbur! Get a load of this: *While I personally am in favour of emerging technologies, and while I personally have nothing against a dress code, I am rather dubious about the effectiveness of the new systems proposed. Statistically speaking, Macdonald Hall has been academically successful with traditional teaching methods. Since this academic success is largely attributable to a traditional approach, it is highly unlikely that such changes will operate for the benefit of the school.*"

"Good old Elmer," said Bruno.

"We can't print that either!" exclaimed Boots. "They'd spot Elmer a block away. And listen to this garbage: *The dress code is interfering with our freedom of expression. It's ruining morale. How can we sit back and watch as the*

*very spirit of Macdonald Hall is crushed by reams of com-
puter code with no feeling for our great tradition? At the
hands of this cyber-monster, our world is crumbling around
us . . . "* His voice trailed off as sudden recognition struck
him.

"Right," said Bruno proudly. "That's mine. No one could
ever guess it came from me."

"*I* did."

"Hey," said Bruno, "Pete Anderson thinks we should
have a jokes and riddles section. Listen: *What rhymes
with drizzle and is ruining Macdonald Hall?"*

"That's idiotic!" cried Boots. "You can't print that!"

"Well, it's better than this wishy-washy stuff," said
Bruno. *"With all due respect to Mr. Wizzle, he may be the
right man, but he is at the wrong school. We realize that he
is a genius when it comes to education . . .* I mean, what's
all that? He isn't a genius at education! He's a jerk at
everything!"

"I wrote that," said Boots. "Listen, if we fill the paper
with a whole lot of articles saying that Mr. Wizzle is an
idiot, the Board isn't going to listen to us. We've got to be
sensible and reasonable."

"Yeah, maybe you're right. Hey, someone's entered a
crossword puzzle. What's a six-letter word for: Dumb guy
who just arrived at Macdonald Hall?"

"We can't use that!"

"Here's a little touch I thought of myself — letters to the
editor. Listen: *Dear Sir, In your May edition . . .* "

"We didn't have a May edition."

"I'm just trying to add a little colour," said Bruno.
"Okay, no letters to the editor. How about some construc-

tive advertising? *Out-of-date school? Need to be brought up to date? Want to be the school of the future? Walter C. Wizzle will have you centuries ahead of the pack. Apply Macdonald Hall. Fullest co-operation promised.* Maybe someone will take him off our hands!"

"Well, maybe," said Boots grudgingly. "Actually, there's no way we can print any of this without making Mr. Wizzle mad. And The Fish too, I'll bet."

"Oh, well," said Bruno, "we'll water it down a bit. How about an advice column? *Dear Sir, I am a student at Macdonald Hall and I used to be happy, but now I'm not anymore. What shall I do? Signed, Wearing a Tie.* Answer: *Dear Wearing a Tie, Get rid of Wizzle.*"

Boots had to laugh. "Bruno, we're going to be expelled!"

* * *

At five-thirty that afternoon Mr. Sturgeon made his way into his house, slipped off his shoes and sat down heavily on the living room sofa.

His wife entered the room. "Hurry up, dear. You just have time for a quick shower and shave. I've invited Mr. Wizzle to dinner."

Mr. Sturgeon's face assumed a pained expression. "I'm tired, Mildred. I had an exhausting day, and the most exhausting thing about it was Wizzle. Why should I have to meet the man socially?"

"Now, dear," said Mrs. Sturgeon, "where's your human kindness?"

"I reserve it for humans."

"William, be serious. Poor Mr. Wizzle is all by himself in the guest cottage. I'm planning to invite him over regularly."

"How regularly?" asked the Headmaster warily.

"I haven't decided yet," his wife replied, "but he's coming tonight. Oh, yes, and I forgot to mention — I've also invited Miss Scrimmage and her administrative assistant, Miss Peabody."

Mr. Sturgeon's face lit up. "Mildred, you're a genius! That's a move that's certain to drive Wizzle into the next county! When that woman from across the road starts talking at him, even WizzleWare won't be able to save him! And her Miss Peabody is probably even worse than she is."

"William, that's a terrible attitude! I want you to be cordial to our guests. It'll be a nice little dinner party."

"I'm not guaranteeing anything. By the way, what's for dinner?"

"We're having a nice fruit salad," said Mrs. Sturgeon cautiously.

"And . . . ?" prompted her husband.

"And cake and coffee."

"But, Mildred, what's the main course?" he persisted.

"The salad, dear. We're not having meat. Mr. Wizzle is a vegetarian."

"But I'm not!"

"It's a simple courtesy. We want Mr. Wizzle to feel welcome, don't we?"

"No, we don't," said Mr. Sturgeon coldly.

"Oh, William, go wash up! And when the guests arrive, be polite!"

* * *

"That was a wonderful dinner, Mrs. Sturgeon," said Mr. Wizzle, leaning back in his chair. "Thank you very much for inviting me."

Mr. Sturgeon was already beginning to feel the first faint stirrings of heartburn that fresh fruit always caused him. "Yes, a wonderful dinner," he agreed sourly.

"So, Miss Peabody," said Mrs. Sturgeon conversationally, "how are you finding Miss Scrimmage's school?"

Miss Peabody snorted into her coffee. "Those girls are so soft it makes me sick!"

Mr. Sturgeon suppressed a smile behind his cup.

"But, Miss Peabody," protested Miss Scrimmage, "of course they're soft! They're young ladies."

"They're pampered, overindulged and overprotected," snapped Miss Peabody, "and it's got to stop. Tomorrow morning at six-thirty the whole school is going to fall in on the front lawn for calisthenics."

Miss Scrimmage was aghast. "But I've always stressed the importance of beauty sleep."

"Balloonjuice!" exclaimed Miss Peabody in disgust.

"My psychological studies," announced Mr. Wizzle, "show clearly that too much emphasis on physical activity takes away from strong study habits. The student becomes exhausted and — "

"Balloonjuice!" repeated Miss Peabody. Mr. Sturgeon chuckled softly.

His wife glared at him. "Would anyone like some more cake?" she offered.

"I'd like another piece, please," said Mr. Wizzle.

"Overindulgence," muttered Miss Peabody.

Mr. Wizzle was determined to be polite. "Miss Peabody, perhaps you'd like to come over and have a look at our new software system. I wrote the code myself — "

"I don't believe in computers," she said flatly. "When

was the last time you saw a computer deliver a good swift kick where it was most needed?"

Miss Scrimmage's cup rattled in its saucer.

"Have some more coffee, Miss Scrimmage," said Mrs. Sturgeon. "Perhaps it will restore you. You look a little pale."

* * *

"Isn't it beautiful?" raved Bruno, holding up the first copy of *The Macdonald Hall Free Press.*

"Yeah, beautiful," agreed Boots, glancing nervously about the print shop. "Let's get out of here. It's one AM!"

"With only one copy?" asked Bruno. "Now, let's see. How many should we run off?"

"Maybe twenty?" suggested Boots.

"Twenty? There are seven hundred guys at Macdonald Hall! We'll print up a thousand just to be on the safe side."

"Bruno, we'll be here all night!" protested Boots.

"That's true," said Bruno. "We'll cut it to five hundred."

"Mark says we can't use more than two hundred and fifty sheets of paper," said Boots. "That'll be plenty. The guys can share them."

"We'll make it three-fifty," decide Bruno. "No one'll know the difference, and there'll be a paper for every two guys. Okay, let's start printing them."

* * *

Cathy Burton lay on her bed, aching in every bone. "I can't believe it!" she gasped. "Six laps! I can't move!"

"Try to relax," suggested Diane solicitously. "We've got to get some sleep. We're going to be up early tomorrow morning for calisthenics."

"Don't worry about that," said Cathy. "I've passed the word. No one's going."

"But Miss Peabody'll be mad!" Diane protested.

Cathy's stiff body tightened a little more. "We don't have to worry about that either. We're getting rid of Miss Peabody. I don't care if it takes us all week — Peabody goes!"

Chapter 4

freedom of the press

Miss Peabody stood, hands on hips, on the lawn in front of Miss Scrimmage's Finishing School for Young Ladies. The girls lay about on the grass in various poses, gasping, choking and sweating.

Cathy's method of passive resistance had not worked. By 6:15, when no students had appeared on the exercise field, Miss Peabody had marched into the residence and, starting with room 1, had physically hauled each girl out of bed.

"You are the most nauseating bunch of cream puffs I've ever seen!" her strident voice rang out. "Look at you! I haven't even worked up a sweat yet! All right, that's enough for now. This afternoon right after classes I want to see every one of you out on the track! Three laps for not showing up on time for calisthenics!"

There were moans of protest.

"Okay, everybody hit the showers before breakfast. Come on! Double time!"

She turned to look across the road where a small group of pajama-clad boys, roused from their sleep, had gathered to investigate the disturbance.

"Hey, you!" she bellowed. "Doesn't Macdonald Hall teach you to mind your own business?"

Pete Anderson nudged Boots. "Who's that?"

Boots shrugged. "Sure isn't Miss Scrimmage in shorts."

* * *

"Instead of beginning our math course today," said Mr. Stratton painfully in Bruno and Boots's first class on Wednesday morning, "I will be passing out some psychological tests which you are to complete. They are not for me, of course. Mr. — uh — Wizzle requires that these be completed in all first classes this morning." He cleared his throat. "These tests have nothing to do with math, and therefore do not have any place here, but — "

"But Mr. Wizzle needs the *feedback*," piped Bruno.

There were general groans and laughter.

"That will do, Walton," said Mr. Stratton with restrained severity. "Now, this is a multiple-choice test. When you decide on your answer, you colour in the appropriate box on the scan sheet. The scan sheets will be evaluated by" — he reddened slightly — "WizzleWare."

Pete Anderson raised his hand. "Sir, how come we're having a test and we haven't even started school yet? What if I don't know the answers?"

"You'll be all right, Anderson," said Mr. Stratton. "These are opinion questions. There are no wrong answers."

The papers were passed out and the testing began. Boots read question one: *In a discussion, your friend takes a stand that is absolutely incorrect. Do you: (a) vehemently contradict him? (b) gently suggest that he reconsider his viewpoint? or (c) let it pass?*

In his mind Boots pictured Bruno pounding tables and ruthlessly pursuing his goals. Contradict? Never. Suggest? What good did it ever do? He filled in *(c)*.

Wilbur Hackenschleimer read over question four. *Your friend needs money to buy a birthday gift for his mother, but all you have is your lunch money. Do you (a) lend him your lunch money? (b) lend him some of your money and have a light lunch? or (c) turn him down outright?* Without hesitation, Wilbur filled in *(c)*. For his part, the question need not have been asked.

Bruno was colouring in squares at random, not even bothering to read the questions. If it were at all possible, he decided, WizzleWare was going to crash over his answers. He paused to admire the nice zigzag pattern his answers formed. Bruno was not in the least worried that his test result might be of any consequence. This was, after all, a Wizzle test.

* * *

Elmer Drimsdale put up his hand. "Sir, how can you make a multiple-choice question out of *Who is the man in history you admire most?* My choice isn't on the list."

Mr. Hubert, Elmer's period one teacher, shook his head impatiently. "Just pick one, Drimsdale. Please."

* * *

Mark Davies, whose first class was phys. ed., lay stretched out on the gym floor, wondering why he had changed into his track shorts in order to fill out papers. *You are invited to a party,* he read, *and you don't know what to wear. Do you: (a) dress formally just in case? (b) risk offending your host by phoning and asking what to wear? or (c) say you have a cold and not go at all?* Mark filled in *(c).* He didn't like parties.

* * *

Pete Anderson chewed on his pencil nervously. *What is your critical opinion of Keats?* Without bothering to read the multiple choice answers, Pete raised his hand. "Mr. Stratton, sir, what's a Keat?"

"I beg your pardon, Anderson?"

"Question three," said Pete. *"What is your critical opinion of Keats?* How can I have a critical opinion? I don't even know what they are!"

Mr. Stratton laughed. "Keats, Anderson! The poet!"

"Oh," said Pete, no better off. "These sure are hard. I think they should have given us a chance to study."

"Just leave it blank and go on to the next one, Anderson. You're far behind and time's almost up."

* * *

Dear Miss Peabody, wrote Cathy Burton, *we at Siberia High School have heard about the marvellous education methods you are using at Miss Scrimmage's Finishing School fur Young Ladies. We will pay you 250,000 rubles a year plus your own polar bear. An immediate reply is requested to Siberia High School, 23 Glacier Avenue, Siberia, Russia. Come at once. You are desperately needed here. Yours truly, Boris Pavlov. P.S. We love doing morning calisthenics.*

"There;" she said aloud. "Siberia should be far enough."

"Do you really think she'll buy that?" asked Diane dubiously.

Cathy shrugged. "Come on. Let's go slip it in her mailbox."

* * *

"Bruno," said Pete Anderson at the lunch table, "do you think we could get rid of Mr. Wizzle before he has a chance to mark those tests?"

"Actually," said Elmer, "it shouldn't take very long to evaluate the tests. They're probably being scanned right now."

"Oh, no!" moaned Pete. "I wonder what happens if you flunk!"

"Don't worry," said Bruno confidently. "Wizzle's as good as gone. Wait till you see the *Free Press!*"

"How did it turn out?" asked Chris. "Were my graphics okay?"

"Fantastic!" Bruno assured him. "The whole paper's a work of art!"

"I've been worried about that all morning," said Boots nervously. "The papers are all sitting in our room. Bruno, you know Wizzle has a passkey. What if he goes snooping around and finds them?"

"No problem," said Bruno. "They won't be there long. Tonight, just after lights-out, we're each going to take a batch and slip them under doors."

Wilbur dropped a cookie. "Hold everything! I'm not risking getting demerits. I got three this morning because Mr. Wizzle saw me eating between classes. Did you know we're not allowed to eat between classes?"

"If you don't help deliver the *Free Press*," warned Bruno,

"Wizzle's going to stay, and then you'll *never* be allowed to eat between classes."

"That's blackmail," accused Wilbur.

"That reminds me," said Mark irritably. "I got three demerits this morning for leaving the print shop in a mess. Thanks a lot, Bruno!"

"I got five demerits last night," said Elmer, shamefaced.

"*You?*" chorused all the boys at the table.

"Yes," Elmer admitted. "Last night the constellation of Orion was so well positioned in the sky that I couldn't resist getting out my telescope, even though it was after lights-out. I was sketching the positions of the stars when, suddenly, they were gone and this huge eye was looking at me."

"I didn't get any demerits," said Larry. "Mr. Wizzle complimented me on my efficiency."

"Your kind causes unrest!" snarled Wilbur.

Elmer sighed nervously. "If I get five more demerits, I'll have to write lines!"

"Oh, no!" Bruno held his head. "My lines! I forgot to hand in my lines! I haven't even got them from Sidney yet!" He ran out of the dining hall.

"That Bruno!" exclaimed Wilbur. "How come he makes everybody do what they don't want to do?"

"It's for our own good," explained Pete. "We have to stop Wizzle before he gives another test!"

Bruno stomped determinedly out of the Faculty Building. Outside he met Boots and Wilbur on their way to afternoon classes.

"I brought your books," said Boots.

"That Wizzle!" stormed Bruno. "Do you know what he

did with those lines? He just scrunched them up and threw them in the garbage! After all Sidney's hard work!"

"What did you expect him to do?" asked Wilbur. "Frame them?"

"And I got five more demerits for being late!" added Bruno. "If demerits were money, I'd be rich!"

"If demerits were brains," said Boots, "you'd behave yourself."

"Look who's talking! You've got five!"

"So what?" Boots defended himself. "Elmer's got five, too. I'm in distinguished company."

"Come on," said Wilbur. "We'll be late for class."

* * *

"Well, Mildred," said Mr. Sturgeon, enjoying a roast beef dinner, "of all the people I might have guessed Miss Scrimmage would hire, that Miss Peabody would be the last."

"What a horrible person," agreed Mrs. Sturgeon. "I feel so sorry for those poor girls."

The Headmaster grimaced. "Those hooligans deserve anything they get. Besides, it could be worse for them. They could have Wizzle. Save your sympathy for our boys. Wizzle gave Drimsdale five demerits last night for having his telescope out after ten PM."

"Well," said his wife, "he was violating curfew. That could interfere with a boy's school work, you know."

"Drimsdale has been a one-man observatory for three years," said the Headmaster, "and never once has his average dropped below ninety-five. Mildred, to give that boy demerits is a crime against science!"

"Mr. Wizzle is new here," Mrs. Sturgeon explained, "and all he saw was a boy breaking the rules."

"I suppose being smarter than Wizzle is against the rules. It would appear that harbouring the smartest boy in the world is one of the things that makes Macdonald Hall a dinosaur."

"Oh dear," said Mrs. Sturgeon. "You think poor Mr. Wizzle is handing out demerits too freely?"

"He is as free with his demerits as he is with his advice," said the Headmaster sourly. "He's called a surprise dormitory inspection for tonight so he can give away even more. Anyway, thank heaven he isn't here for dinner again. Pass the meat, please."

"William, your attitude is deplorable," scolded Mrs. Sturgeon. "In no time at all I'm sure Mr. Wizzle will fit nicely into Macdonald Hall."

"Mr. Wizzle will fit nicely into the furnace," replied her husband evenly.

"I didn't hear that, William!"

* * *

Bruno patted the stack of newspapers lovingly. "Ten minutes to ten. At five after, we start distributing."

Boots was having second thoughts. "You know, some of these articles are pretty rough on Mr. Wizzle. Like this one, where it says his ideas serve no useful purpose here. Or this pros and cons chart where it says 'Nil' under the pros. He's going to be really mad!"

"Well," said Bruno hopefully, "maybe he'll just go away without being too insulted."

There was a sharp rap on the door.

"Who is it?" called Bruno.

"Dormitory inspection," called the voice of Walter C. Wizzle.

Boots grabbed the stack of papers and began to run around the room in panic.

"Out the window!" whispered Bruno. Aloud he called, "Coming, Mr. Wizzle, sir."

Boots threw open the window and dumped *The Macdonald Hall Free Press* into the bushes. He slammed the window shut just as Bruno opened the door to admit Mr. Wizzle, followed by a grim-looking Mr. Sturgeon.

Notebook poised, Mr. Wizzle looked around the room with a critical eye. "Oh, yes, Walton and O'Neal, isn't it?"

"Y–yessir," stammered Boots.

"Well . . . not yet ready for bed — two demerits. Hmmm . . . very untidy room, disgracefully so — three demerits. Beds not properly made — one more demerit. There is no food in here, is there?"

"No, sir," said Bruno, "no food."

"Good." Mr. Wizzle nodded. "There's one student in this dormitory who had his entire desk filled to the brim with groceries. I had to confiscate three cartons."

"You took away Wilbur's food?" blurted Boots.

The Headmaster turned away to cough.

Mr. Wizzle consulted his notebook. "Six demerits each. Well, O'Neal, that gives you eleven. Two hundred lines — *I will obey fully all the rules of Macdonald Hall.* Walton, two hundred and fifty from you. On my desk. Friday morning." He gave the room a last glance. "And clean this room up. That's all." He turned and left. The Headmaster followed, tossing over his shoulder a glance that neither Bruno nor Boots could decipher.

"Walter C. Wizzle!" muttered Bruno as the door shut

behind Mr. Sturgeon. "Four hundred and fifty lines between the two of us!"

"We never had any surprise inspections before," said Boots bitterly. "We were too lenient in those articles!" His jaw dropped. *"The papers!"*

The two boys rushed to the window and heaved it open. An awful sight met their eyes. A brisk wind had come up and all three hundred and fifty copies of *The Macdonald Hall Free Press* were strewn over the campus.

"Bruno, look!" cried Boots in horror.

Bruno laughed diabolically. "There's our distribution. Everybody's bound to get a copy, including Wizzle. Let's not bother writing those lines. By the time Friday rolls around, Wizzle will be packed and gone!"

* * *

"Look," said Diane reasonably, "if you hadn't tried to get out of running the three laps, you wouldn't have got all those others."

"It's war, that's what it is!" wailed Cathy. "We'll show her!"

"Cathy, if I were you, I'd think twice about starting a war with a Marine."

With effort, Cathy sat up in her bed. "Think about what you're saying! Peabody may be a professional monster, but we're Miss Scrimmage's Finishing School for Young Ladies! Think of all the stuff we've done! The riot squad is afraid to come back here! We're *somebody!*"

"If we try to go against Peabody," warned Diane, "we're somebody dead."

"She's got the power," conceded Cathy, "but we've got the numbers. She's outnumbered three hundred to one. Surely we can beat her!"

Chapter 5

the dividing line

"Boy," sighed Mark Davies over the lunch table, "was Wizzle ever mad! He asked me if I printed the paper and I said no. Then he asked me if I wrote the articles and I said no. Then he asked if I knew who did and I didn't answer, so he gave me ten demerits for not answering. I've got to do two hundred lines! Listen, Bruno, the next time you get a brilliant idea, use someone else's printing press!"

"At least he got the message," said Bruno, pleased.

"He got the message, all right," said Boots. "At this morning's assembly I thought he was going to kill all of us. The Fish didn't look too pleased either."

"I got lines last night," muttered Wilbur sourly. "Boy, did I get zonked at dorm inspection! He took away all my food and left eight demerits. Now I've got eleven."

Chris Talbot joined the conversation. "Pete and I picked up three demerits for having a messy room. Our room isn't messy!"

"And it doesn't look like Wizzle is going away," added Larry. "I overheard him talking to a member of the Board, complaining about the *Free Press*. He raved about how immature and irresponsible we are, and he said he was taking down his input boxes because we were too childish to merit them. And he said he's staying."

"Hey, Larry," asked Pete, "do you have any idea what's going on at Scrimmage's? They're doing nothing but phys. ed. over there, and there's this lady with a real loud voice."

Larry shrugged. "The word is that Miss Scrimmage has a new assistant. That must be her."

"It's unreal," confirmed Boots. "She's running around there at dawn barking orders like a drill sergeant. I feel sorry for the girls."

There was a loud crash behind them. "Hi, guys. I'm out." Sidney Rampulsky gathered up the things that had fallen from his tray, put his lunch down on the table and sat down beside Mark, his roommate.

"Welcome back, Sidney," Bruno greeted him. "Did you get a copy of *The Macdonald Hall Free Press*?"

"Yeah, I was reading it on my way over here and I bumped into Mr. Wizzle. He gave me five demerits just for having a copy! But I think he was mad because when I fell, he went down, too."

"Did you fall again?" stormed Mark.

"This time it's okay," grinned Bruno. "He fell on Wizzle.

All right, you guys, when should we publish the next *Free Press*?"

"Never!" chorused everyone.

Bruno pounded the table. "Well, come on, then. We need ideas on how to get rid of Wizzle. Are you just going to sit there and let him walk all over you?"

"Yes!" chorused everyone.

"What?" cried Bruno.

"Look," said Chris Talbot. "Wizzle's really mad. As it is, he's taken away the whole school's off-campus privileges indefinitely."

"Yeah," said Mark, "and my paper is shut down. If something else happens, Wizzle's going to start expelling people."

"But we can't let little things like that scare us," protested Bruno.

"Being expelled is not a little thing," put in Boots. "It goes on your record for good."

"Not to mention that your parents kill you," added Pete. "I have enough trouble explaining my grades."

"Gee, Bruno," said Sidney, "I don't like Wizzle very much, but I don't want to risk getting expelled." There was general agreement all around.

"Besides," said Larry, "if we all keep our noses clean, the only problem will be the dress code, and we'll just have to get used to that."

Bruno's eyes reflected deep pain. "But what's the point of having a committee if we don't do anything?"

"Well," said Wilbur, "I guess we don't have a committee, then."

Bruno leapt to his feet. "You're darn right we have a

committee! As long as there's a Macdonald Hall, there's always a committee! I don't care if you all walk out! Boots and I are still on the committee!"

Boots turned to his roommate and best friend to deliver the message that had been in his mind all day. "Not me, Bruno. I'm out. I'm sorry. I think it's great that you have so much school spirit, but this is the end of the line. It's just too dangerous."

"Come on, guys," said Larry. "We've got to get to classes."

They got up and moved out of the dining hall, leaving Bruno all alone, staring at the empty chairs.

* * *

"Look at this, Mildred," chuckled the Headmaster over the breakfast table. "It's the greatest cartoon I've ever seen!" In the middle of *The Macdonald Hall Free Press* was a drawing of a computer with evil eyes, sharp teeth and a menacing expression. Around its neck was a wide tie clearly marked *WizzleWare*. The tie acted as a leash, and was being held by a little man wearing a T-shirt that said *Call Me Wiz.* In the foreground was the Faculty Building of Macdonald Hall. The computer was spewing a dark cloud, which hung over it.

"I don't think it's funny," said Mrs. Sturgeon. "It's disrespectful and rude. The boys should be punished. It's too bad you don't know who is responsible."

The Headmaster laughed. "Certainly I know. The cartoon — Talbot, of course. The boy certainly has talent. And this headline *Sanctity of Macdonald Hall Threatened* — that's obviously Walton. I recognize his flair for the dramatic. This cautious one here is O'Neal — gets right to the point, he does. The intelligent one is Drimsdale, the one about ties inhibiting the intake of food is obviously Hackenschleimer, and there are assorted tidbits from Anderson, Wilson and Rampulsky."

"They should be punished," his wife repeated. "Poor Mr. Wizzle."

"On the contrary, Mildred," said Mr. Sturgeon seriously, "I think this newspaper is quite an accomplishment. That's what education is about, after all — to encourage independent thought and self-expression. Our boys have every right to express their own opinions about how this school is run."

"If they were complaining about *you*, you wouldn't be so complacent," accused Mrs. Sturgeon. "Poor Mr. Wizzle will be so upset!"

"If you had seen him dishing out demerits last night, you wouldn't be quite so sympathetic. He's antagonizing the boys and they're not intending to take it lying down. I don't blame them at all. Mildred, I'm in a very difficult position. I never liked Wizzle and I always considered him and his ideas a nuisance. But now things are serious. The boys aren't happy here at Macdonald Hall anymore. And Wizzle is so angry over this newspaper that if anything else like it ever happens he's liable to start talking about expulsion. And the Board just might go along with him. That certainly isn't what we want at Macdonald Hall."

"I can see your point," his wife conceded. "Is there anything you can do privately to calm the boys down a little?"

"Mildred, be realistic. As Headmaster I have to support Board decisions, and Wizzle is a Board decision." He smiled wryly. "And while I'm mentioning that the boys aren't content, I guess I'd be less than honest if I didn't admit that I don't like being a lame-duck Headmaster. I haven't made an administrative decision yet this year. Wizzle does all that."

"Oh dear. And the boys really don't like Mr. Wizzle."

Mr. Sturgeon sighed. "I'm afraid, Mildred, there are hard times ahead."

* * *

"Miss Peabody," said Miss Scrimmage timidly over tea in the Headmistress's sitting room, "don't you think you're being a little harsh with the girls? All those laps? And calisthenics again this morning?"

"Absolutely not," replied Miss Peabody. "Those girls are much too soft. But just give me a little more time with them." She produced Cathy's letter and chuckled at the mere memory. "One of them wants to get rid of me so badly that she sent me a job offer from Russia written in green ink on pink stationery. Now, that's funny! Oh, I am enjoying it here!"

"Really?" said Miss Scrimmage. "From the way you act — all the shouting and screaming — I would have guessed that you were quite unhappy."

"The girls need it," said Miss Peabody firmly.

"Well," sighed Miss Scrimmage, "I always like to think that the girls are fond of me."

Miss Peabody looked at her pityingly. "I always like to think that the girls are *scared* of me."

* * *

Boots returned to room 306 after class that afternoon, his footsteps heavy. In all their classes together, Bruno had ignored him totally. Feeling exhausted, Boots put his key in the lock and opened the door. His jaw dropped.

Right down the centre of the room was a thick line of masking tape. It divided the two beds, dressers and desks, and all Boots's possessions that had been placed in Bruno's part of the room were now piled on the bed by the window.

Bruno was lying on his bed staring thoughtfully up at the ceiling.

"Bruno, what's all this?"

Bruno did not turn his head. "Just be glad that you're still staying in the room. I had your bags packed and outside the door, but Wizzle came along and slapped me with five demerits for making a mess in the hall. That ought to please you. You're a big Wizzle fan."

"You know I'm not a Wizzle fan. I'm just — "

"Anyway," Bruno went on, "since we seem to be doomed to room together, you stick to your half and I'll stick to mine. Right now your feet are on my half. Shove off."

"How come the bathroom and the closet are in your half? Not to mention the door."

"First come, first served," said Bruno. "You can use all three — especially the door."

"Bruno, this just isn't like you."

"Oh, it's a lot like me. You're the one who's changed. And when you abandoned Macdonald Hall, I abandoned you."

"I haven't abandoned Macdonald Hall," snapped Boots. "But when I do, it won't be with my suitcase under my arm and my expulsion papers in my hand!"

"I'm not leaving at all," said Bruno. "Wizzle is leaving. Now I've said all I intend to say to you. Get over on your own side."

It was almost 2 AM when Cathy Burton put her ear up to the door of Miss Peabody's room and signalled that the Assistant Headmistress was asleep.

Five other girls came out of the shadows. As quietly as they could, the group pushed a long table right in front of the doorway. Then they jammed two chairs underneath the table and placed another smaller table upside down atop the first. Three more chairs were added to the top of this structure, and assorted night tables, chairs, piano stools and serving carts were placed strategically in the corridor, effectively blocking off Miss Peabody's door.

The girls rushed around the corner and stopped for a last-minute briefing.

"Are you sure all the girls know?" asked Cathy.

The five nodded.

"Okay. It all happens at two. Sergeant Peabody will rue the day she ever tried to match wits with Miss Scrimmage's Finishing School for Young Ladies!"

* * *

Bruno Walton had not been able to get to sleep. In spite of his air of confident determination, he was disheartened. He was disappointed in his friends, especially Boots, for abandoning Macdonald Hall like this, and had decided to go for help to a source he was sure would not fail him.

He tossed a handful of pebbles up to the second-storey window. Diane's white face appeared. Her hand waved frantically and pointed toward Macdonald Hall. Bruno shrugged, shinnied up the drainpipe and climbed into the room.

"Go home, Bruno!" whispered Diane frantically.

"Why? What's wrong? Where's Cathy?"

"Cathy's at war!" replied Diane, wringing her hands in anxiety. "Oh, Bruno, you have no idea what's been going on here!"

"Well, I know there's some lady making you do exercises."

"Oh, she's a monster!" shrilled Diane. "Which is why you've got to get out of here! Any second now — "

The fire bell went off with an ear-splitting clang.

"Oh," grinned Bruno. "It's a riot. Why didn't you say so in the first place?"

Diana covered her eyes and whimpered.

Bruno grabbed her by the arm and ran out into the residence hall. It was full of girls, fully dressed, screaming, banging doors and making as much noise as possible as they headed for the exits. Suddenly the corridor lights went out.

"What's going on?" bellowed Bruno, stumbling in the darkness, the bell still clanging in his ears. He grabbed the person nearest to him. It was Cathy.

"Oh, hi," she greeted him. "How are you?"

Bruno and the girls thundered down the stairs and out the front door onto the lawn. He turned to see a crowd of boys from Macdonald Hall swarming across the highway, coming to the girls' rescue.

"Where's Miss Peabody?" shouted Cathy.

"Yeah! Where's Miss Peabody?" echoed someone.

"Who's Miss Peabody?" shouted half the Macdonald Hall crowd.

"Shut up and rescue, stupid! Can't you see there's a fire going on?"

Miss Scrimmage burst out the front door, shining her flashlight into people's faces and waving her shotgun in the air. "Girls! Girls! Don't panic!"

"Stay where you are!" Mr. Wizzle was shouting. "Stay where you are, or you'll all get demerits!"

Mr. Sturgeon ran into the scene, dressed in his red silk bathrobe and bedroom slippers. "Put the gun down, Miss Scrimmage!" he called nervously, convinced from past experience that even a fire was not as dangerous as the Headmistress with her shotgun. He began to make his way through the surging crowd toward Miss Scrimmage. There, in a crowd of girls, prancing, shouting and rioting with the best of them, was Bruno Walton.

"Walton," said Mr. Sturgeon, quietly, but clearly.

Bruno wheeled. "Oh! — uh — hello, sir."

"Walton, is there a fire here?"

"Well, actually, sir," said Bruno, "I don't think so."

"Then what," asked the Headmaster amidst the screaming voices of the girls, the shouting of the boys and the loud clanging of the fire bell, "is the *meaning* of all this?"

Onto the front balcony burst Gloria Peabody, eyes blazing. She cupped her hands to her mouth. "Atten-*hut*!!!"

There was instant, deafening silence, broken only by the insistent clanging of the fire bell. Everyone froze.

"Now," she shouted, her strong voice carrying across the lawn even to the apple orchard, where some of the students were perched in the trees, "everyone from Macdonald Hall, *scram!*"

"Oh, Miss Peabody," called out Mr. Wizzle. "Could I please have a word — "

"You've had it! The word was scram!"

The boys from Macdonald Hall turned and ran across the highway, their teachers hot on their heels. Even Mr. Sturgeon, struggling to maintain his dignity, scurried across the road, slippers flapping.

The girls of Miss Scrimmage's stood frozen in terror, staring up at the balcony, waiting for the boom to descend on them.

"You'll be sorry you lost this sleep!" Miss Peabody thundered. "Calisthenics are at six-thirty, as usual! After class you're all going to run laps!" She paused. All that could be heard was the fire alarm, still ringing. "And someone turn that racket off!"

Miss Scrimmage scurried into the building and in a few moments the alarm was silent.

A number of cars had stopped on the soft shoulder of the highway, and several helpful motorists came forward to offer their assistance.

"Get out of here! Mind your own business!"

A baffled driver turned to Cathy. "Is this a school?"

"Not anymore," she said bitterly. "It's an army camp."

Chapter 6

an earth-shaking idea

For days following the riot, things were quiet at Macdonald Hall. Bruno, still miffed at being deserted by his committee, ate all his meals alone and lived behind a wall of silence. Mr. Wizzle, finding Bruno fully dressed at Scrimmage's the night of the riot, had assumed him to be at the heart of the disturbance. The cost: ten demerits, which, coupled with two he had picked up for being seen outside without his tie, brought his total to forty-one. In spite of his isolation, he was never lonely, since all his time was spent writing lines.

Boots, along with most of the boys at Macdonald Hall, was doing his very best to stay out of Mr. Wizzle's way and avoid getting any more demerits. Boots was not happy, however, because Bruno was still angry, still having nothing to do with him. He was finding the silence in the divided room 306 awfully hard to bear. And the scratching of Bruno's pen grinding out hundreds of punishment lines did nothing to alleviate the tension.

Meanwhile, Mr. Wizzle was hard at work redesigning the curriculum of Macdonald Hall, sometimes to the shock of the students, always to the dismay of the teachers.

It was a week after the big riot. Mr. Sturgeon was walking down the basement stairs of the Faculty Building and accidentally came upon his entire teaching staff beneath the stairs, crowded around a dusty card table. The Headmaster raised an eyebrow. "Don't I get invited to staff meetings anymore?"

Mr. Stratton flushed. "Well, William, we were just having a little discussion about — uh — Wizzle."

Mr. Sturgeon smiled lightly. "It didn't look much like a poker game. But is it a revolution?"

"He's trying to tell me how to teach gym!" blurted Coach Flynn angrily. "He couldn't manage a deep knee bend if he practised for a week! Uh — I mean, he doesn't have the experience and — "

"I know what you mean, Alex," said the Headmaster. "Any other comments?"

There was a babble of voices.

"One at a time, please."

Mr. Hubert stroked his beard in exasperation. "He wants me to teach chemistry by computer, so he wrote a program in his blasted WizzleWare to simulate an experiment. He spent the whole class downloading it on my PC, which crashed the second he clicked *Install*. Now he wants me to hold up my lessons until he can get it up and working. What are we supposed to do in the meantime? Make fudge?"

"One of my students has stopped paying attention in class and spends all his time writing lines. He's been at it for days."

"You have Walton, too, eh?" said Mr. Stratton. "Wizzle insists that when I teach math I have to explain to my students the practical applications of what we're doing. I told him to go ahead and he went right up there and told the boys they have to know algebra because at any time in later life they may be called upon to factor a polynomial by completing the square. They all laughed in his face and he gave a class detention and demerits all around."

"The English Department has a more serious grievance," said Mr. Foley, tight-lipped. "Mr. Wizzle has eliminated practically everything that we do."

"At least you've got a department," said Mr. Fudge, the guidance counsellor. "Wizzle has taken over mine. That WizzleWare has a program to psychoanalyze the students, and you wouldn't believe what it's come up with."

Mr. Sturgeon held up his hands for silence. "Enough. I've been bringing matters like this before the Board ever since Mr. Wizzle got here. They are a hundred percent sure he's a genius, so my hands are tied. We'll just have to tolerate the situation and do our best to teach under the circumstances." He smiled thinly. "I suppose it could be worse."

"Yeah," blurted Flynn, "we could be at Scrimmage's. I hear Peabody decided to retrain their phys. ed. teacher and now she's at Toronto General recuperating from near-fatal exhaustion."

There was a chorus of laughter. Mr. Sturgeon sighed.

* * *

At Miss Scrimmage's the atmosphere was just as tense. From reveille at 6 AM to taps at 10 PM, Miss Peabody's reign of terror rolled on.

When she was not running laps, Cathy Burton was waging war on the new Assistant Headmistress. She could still recall her conversation with Miss Peabody the morning after the big riot.

"You're going to run a lot of laps for causing that ruckus last night, Burton."

"But Miss Peabody," Cathy had protested innocently, "you've got no proof that I had anything to do with it!"

"I've got all the proof I need, Burton — a gut feeling that you did it."

Cathy grinned in spite of herself at the memory of Diane coming back from the cleanup detail outside Miss Peabody's room.

"Remember all that furniture you piled up there?" Diane had gasped. "Splinters! Toothpicks! Sawdust! Peabody's a juggernaut! She must know karate or something!"

Miss Peabody had stomped around the corner just then. "It was jiu-jitsu. I learned it in the Marines." Then she had assigned two laps for each of them.

Cathy had spent her sparse amount of free time that week releasing field mice into Miss Peabody's room, short-sheeting her bed, greasing her floor and over-spicing her food. All of these things met with a degree of success that matched the number of laps Cathy was slapped with. She had even placed a tape recorder in the Assistant Headmistress's room. While Miss Peabody slept, it played over and over again the words: "Tomorrow you will be sweet and nice and kind and not rotten at all." But the next day Miss Peabody had been worse than ever, complaining of a restless night and terrible dreams.

Miss Scrimmage, meanwhile, was too terrified to interfere. She had taken to spending all her time reading in her sitting room. Miss Peabody was in charge.

* * *

While Boots was out at track and field practice, Bruno, as always, sat at his desk finishing up the very last of his lines.

There was a sharp knock at the door.

"Go away!" growled Bruno, who didn't feel like seeing anyone. "I'm busy!"

The knocking resumed, louder and more persistent.

"Oh, all right!" Bruno got up and opened the door. There stood Elmer Drimsdale, his crew cut in disarray, his glasses awry, his tie undone. His face was flushed, and his eyes were rolling strangely.

"Elmer, what happened to you?"

Elmer stormed into the room, slamming the door behind him. "Bruno, I am incensed!"

"Yeah, I know that," said Bruno incredulously. The normally placid, timid Elmer, who never raised his voice above a whisper, was waving his arms and shouting.

"Are you aware of what happened last night! *Are you aware of what happened last night?*"

"Calm down, Elmer. How could I be? What happened?"

"All right, I'll tell you what happened!" stormed Elmer. "It was an incredibly clear night last night and I had my telescope focused on globular cluster M-13 in the constellation Hercules. It was wonderful. Everything was so clear . . . " A dreamy look passed over Elmer's face. "Then Mr. Wizzle caught me. He confiscated my telescope and searched my room! He took away my microscope and all my bacterial cultures! He emptied my bathtub and completely ruined my mollusc experiment! My hybrid grain experiment went, too, along with most of my plants and all my data! He even took my ant colony! Oh, I'm so mad! I have twenty demerits now! I have to write lines! How demeaning! How stultifying! If I were a violent person, I would kick something!"

"Go right ahead," Bruno invited.

Elmer reared back and delivered Boots's bed a mighty kick.

"Feel better?"

"No!" Elmer hopped around the room cradling his foot. "I think I've injured all my metatarsals! Bruno, I have concluded that being expelled is nothing compared with being deprived of my experiments! I want you to help me remove Mr. Wizzle from Macdonald Hall!"

Bruno's face broke into a wide grin. "Now you're talking! Wizzle must go!"

"Indisputably!" stormed Elmer. "And we'll start immediately — as soon as we stop by at the infirmary and see about my foot."

"Right," grinned Bruno. "We'll work in your room — I don't want Boots to know what we're doing."

* * *

"He really cleaned the place out," said Bruno, surveying room 201, in which Elmer lived alone.

"Yes," agreed Elmer forlornly. "It seems so empty. I never realized what good company my ants were."

"Hey, Elmer," said Bruno, pointing at a large grey box with an enormous circular cone speaker, "I didn't know you had a sound system."

"It's not a sound system," said Elmer. "Mr. Wizzle thought it was, too, and I didn't disabuse him of the notion, so he left it here."

"What is it?"

"It's a low-frequency audio generator," explained Elmer. "It makes subsonic sounds at very high decibels, but it can't be heard because the sounds are too low."

"What good is a sound system that you can't hear?"

"It's just an interest of mine," said Elmer. "I've been experimenting with it."

"What does it do?"

"Well, it can simulate a small earth tremor."

Bruno's eyes popped. "You made an *earthquake machine?*"

"Well, I suppose on a very small scale, yes. The sound produced is between eight and nine cycles per second. It is largely inaudible, but will produce overtones in the form of a low rumble. I'm just experimenting with it now, leaving it on for very short periods of time. If left on too long, it could conceivably do some damage."

"Can it work somewhere else besides here?" asked Bruno.

"Yes, of course. It can be operated from a distance by remote control."

"Great!" cried Bruno, grinning broadly. "Tonight Wizzle's getting this in his basement!"

"What for?" asked Elmer.

"Just to shake him up a little," said Bruno. "If it won't drive him away, at least it'll drive him nuts!"

Just after midnight, a tapping at the window of room 306 brought Boots out of a light sleep. He raised the window to admit Cathy and Diane.

"You guys have *got* to save us!" Cathy was moaning, even as Boots was helping her and Diane into the room. "We've got to get rid of that monster! Hey, where's Bruno?"

"I don't know," mumbled Boots.

"What do you mean you don't know? *Where's Bruno?*"

"I think he's out with Elmer Drimsdale," said Boots lamely.

"What do you mean you *think*?" shrilled Cathy. Her sharp eyes spotted the tape that divided the room. "What's going on here?"

"Bruno hasn't spoken to me ever since I quit his committee," explained Boots dully.

"You quit Bruno's committee?" echoed Diane incredulously.

"Wizzle's here to stay," said Boots, "but Bruno won't accept that fact. He's going to get himself and everyone around him expelled, and that's where I draw the line."

"You're knuckling under!" accused Cathy. "That's terrible! What would happen if *I* knuckled under?"

"We'd run a lot fewer laps," said Diane feelingly.

Cathy ignored her. "Poor Bruno! Boots, how could you? He's out there trying to help everyone, working all alone— "

A dark shape appeared at the window and Bruno climbed inside. "I tell you, Elm," he was saying, "Wizzle's as good as gone."

Elmer Drimsdale was climbing into the room behind him. "Well, it certainly will teach him a lesson, Bruno. Imagine confiscating my experiments! Actually, I found the danger of this evening rather exhilarating. I mean, breaking into Mr. Wizzle's basement — "

"Shhh! Elm, we can't let you-know-who know about what we're doing!"

"But you can tell us," chimed in Cathy. "Hi, guys. What's up? And can we use it, too?"

Elmer Drimsdale went immediately mute, as he always did in the presence of females.

"Oh, hi." Bruno beamed. "I can't say too much about it, but we're using science against Wizzle."

"Can we have some science, too?" begged Cathy. "Like maybe a disintegration ray?"

"Or anything that has a chance against jiu-jitsu?" added Diane hopefully.

"Gee, I sure wish I could help you," said Bruno. "Of course, we're a little understaffed here." He looked pointedly across the room at Boots.

"I'm not listening," muttered Boots.

"Why don't you go to Miss Scrimmage?" suggested Bruno.

"We tried that," said Cathy. "She's more scared of Peabody than we are. She spends most of her time in hiding."

"So what?" said Bruno. "It's Miss Scrimmage's school."

"And Macdonald Hall is The Fish's school. What's The Fish doing for you?"

"I see your point," said Bruno. "I can't really figure out what The Fish thinks of all this Wizzle business."

"None of this helps us with Peabody," insisted Diane, "and it's getting late. Come on, Cathy, let's go."

"Why don't you try the softer approach?" suggested Bruno. "Get the whole school together and have a cry in."

"That's a great idea!" exclaimed Cathy. "Peabody's so military that she probably doesn't know how to deal with tears! And we can give her buckets of them!"

The girls left and Elmer, his voice restored, whispered, "Shouldn't we go over to my room? Aren't we going to test the — ?"

"Shhh, Elm!" With his thumb, Bruno motioned toward Boots. "Okay, let's go."

"I hope nobody minds if I go to bed," called Boots sarcastically.

* * *

Walter C. Wizzle was sleeping when the feeling came over him. It was a shaking, a vibration that he felt from deep within his body. He sat bolt upright in bed and looked about the darkened room. Perhaps it was something he'd eaten.

He went to the bathroom to search for a stomach remedy and noticed that the toothbrush was trembling in its glass, the shower doors were shaking, the soap was vibrating in its dish. Even the floor under his feet seemed to be — what was that? Yes, there was a distant roar. What was going on here?

He ran out into the hall. All the fixtures were rattling too, and all the pictures on the wall. He ran into the small kitchen. All the crockery was clacking together. He opened the refrigerator door. A dozen eggs slopped down onto the floor.

Suddenly the roar stopped and the rattling ceased. He rushed to the window and looked at all the other buildings. The whole campus was in darkness. No one else was up. How strange!

Chapter 7

double fault

Bruno Walton sat beside Elmer Drimsdale in second period class, geography. Mr. Thomas, the teacher, was lecturing on the earth's crust formation. Mr. Wizzle sat at the back of the class, making elaborate notes.

" . . . and that's all. Are there any questions?"

Bruno elbowed Elmer.

Elmer stood up. "Sir, I would like to make a special presentation to the class."

Everyone groaned. Elmer's special presentations were notorious at Macdonald Hall.

"By all means. Go ahead, Drimsdale," said Mr. Thomas.

Elmer walked to the front of the class and set up several charts and sketches along the blackboard ledge. "My project deals with the Great Lakes–St. Lawrence Lowlands fault line."

Mr. Thomas frowned. "What fault line?"

"The earthquake fault line, sir," replied Elmer blandly.

At the back of the room Wizzle's head snapped up to attention.

"The Great Lakes–St. Lawrence Lowlands fault line is not as well known as the San Andreas fault line in California, but nevertheless it exists, representing a clear and present danger to the area. The fault itself has been dormant since the Lower Cretaceous Period. However, a hairline offshoot of the fault, which I have named the Elmer Drimsdale fault because I pinpointed it, is quite active. The end of this line actually extends to the Macdonald Hall grounds, passing directly underneath the south lawn."

Now Elmer had Mr. Wizzle's full attention. That strange incident last night! An earthquake!

"Seismic activity has been rather light of late," Elmer went on, "but if you refer to this chart, you can see that a quake of major proportions is overdue."

"Remarkable," said Mr. Thomas. "Is Macdonald Hall then in danger?"

"Oh, no," said Elmer. "You see, activity on my fault line is very local. Even in the event of a major seismic disturbance, the nearby buildings would remain intact." He paused and beamed. "Naturally, however, there would be complete and utter devastation on the fault line itself. Now this map has all the Macdonald Hall buildings plotted. The red line is the Elmer Drimsdale fault. As you can see, all dormitories and educational buildings are located a safe distance from the fault. The only one that lies on it is — uh — the guest cottage."

All the boys wheeled to stare at Mr. Wizzle, who pocketed his notebook and left the room, looking quite pale.

"Elmer," whispered Bruno, "I love you!"

* * *

Mr. Sturgeon leaned back in his chair. "What can I do for you, Wizzle?"

"I'll come right to the point, Mr. Sturgeon. I'd like to talk to you about the earthquake fault my house is built on."

Mr. Sturgeon's eyes opened wide. "Do tell."

"Yes, well, I just heard that my cottage is located on an earthquake fault and —"

"Excuse me, Wizzle," said the Headmaster, "but where did you hear this?"

Mr. Wizzle thought of Elmer Drimsdale's impeccable scholastic reputation. "From a very reliable source."

"I've been Headmaster here for almost twenty years," said Mr. Sturgeon, "and we have never had an earthquake."

"Oh, really?" challenged Mr. Wizzle. "Well, I had one last night."

"Funny. I didn't notice anything."

"That's because your house isn't on the fault."

"That's absurd," said the Headmaster. "Your house is no more than twenty-five metres from mine."

"It's a very local fault," insisted Mr. Wizzle. "My source even said so."

"I see. What else did your source say?"

"He said that we were long overdue for a major earthquake. Frankly, I'm wondering if the cottage is safe."

Mr. Sturgeon raised an eyebrow. "Well, if you're really that frightened, Wizzle, I'm sure we can arrange other accommodations — perhaps a small spare room in one of the dormitories."

Mr. Wizzle bristled. "I'm not at all frightened. I simply wanted to give you some input on this matter." He turned on his heel and stalked out.

The Headmaster reached for the telephone and dialled his home number. "Mildred? . . . You've got to hear what Wizzle's done this time . . . No, it's not mean. It's funny . . ."

* * *

Cathy and Diane sat amid Miss Scrimmage's student body while Miss Peabody addressed the assembly.

"Now remember," whispered Cathy, "as soon as she says something mean, start crying."

"She never says anything that *isn't* mean."

"I meant something *really* mean. Don't forget, cry loud. When the girls hear us, they'll all start, too. I don't want a dry eye in the place."

"Now," Miss Peabody was saying, "there's been a little improvement since I came, but you are still the most nauseating, miserable bunch of softies —"

"Waaah!" Cathy wailed at top volume.

Diane joined in with a series of sobs like hiccups. And one by one the entire student body burst into uncontrolled tears, until the whole gymnasium echoed with sobbing, wailing, crying, shrieking and howling voices.

Miss Scrimmage leapt up from her chair and began running back and forth in front of the assembly. "Girls! Girls! Please don't cry! Oh dear! Don't cry! Miss Peabody didn't mean it! *Please* don't cry!"

This encouraged the girls, who cried harder. Miss Peabody stood at the front of the group, arms folded, glancing dispassionately at her wristwatch.

After a full five minutes, the wailing began to diminish. Cathy looked. Miss Peabody was still there, staring at her watch.

"Waaah!" Cathy howled, and the crying swelled again.

"Oh dear! Oh dear!" agonized Miss Scrimmage. "Miss Peabody, what shall we do?" She looked desperately at the sea of red faces and burst into tears herself.

Miss Peabody remained unmoved. After another five minutes, voices began to grow hoarse and, slowly but surely, the wailing petered out. Cathy kept crying to rally the girls, but finally the last echo of her wailing bounced off the walls and the room fell into total silence.

Miss Peabody stepped forward and fixed them all with a look that would have melted lead. "Are you quite finished with that blubbering?"

The only reply was the sound of Miss Scrimmage blowing her nose.

"I'll see you all out on the track this afternoon. You wasted ten good minutes! Ten good laps should cover it.

"Now, I want to tell you about our new program. You girls lack spirit, excitement and initiative. That's why I'm dividing up the whole school into four squadrons by last names. A to G — Blue Squadron; H to L — Red Squadron; M to R — Green Squadron; S to Z — White Squadron. Now, instead of calisthenics in the morning I'll be teaching you how to march. Then you're on your own to practice and get ready for Saturday's parade."

There was an alarmed murmur.

"Stow it! The squadron that presents the best parade gets an overnight trip somewhere or other with Miss Scrimmage. Okay, that's all. Dismissed. See you on the track."

As the girls began to file out of the gym, Cathy leaned over to Diane. "Did you hear that? A trip with Miss Scrimmage! That means a trip without Peabody!"

"Overnight!" added Diane wistfully.

Cathy's face took on a look of determination. "We're going to win that parade! I'd do anything for a twenty-four-hour pass!"

* * *

Mr. Wizzle ushered Wilbur Hackenschleimer briskly into his office. "Well, Hacken, and how are you today?"

Wilbur looked at him. "That's Hackenschleimer, sir."

"Yes, that's exactly what I wanted to talk to you about. Hackenschleimer — that's fifteen letters. WizzleWare doesn't like that. Our programs conserve memory for improved processing speed. Twelve letters is the maximum. I've decided to shorten your name down to Hacken."

Wilbur was taken aback. "But, sir, we've always been Hackenschleimer!"

"It's all in the interests of efficiency, Hacken," said Mr. Wizzle. "Besides, I think it has quite a nice ring to it. Wilbur Hacken. Yes. When you turn eighteen you should seriously consider having it changed permanently. Well, that's settled then."

Wilbur's face was red. "But, sir —"

"No buts, Hacken. That's all. You can go. Try to cut down on the eating, will you? Good day."

Big Wilbur Hackenschleimer stormed out of the office. By the time he stepped out of the Faculty Building he was running, and when he reached Dormitory 3 his pounding footsteps were shaking the ground. He entered the building, stormed down the hall and burst unannounced into room 306. Boots was out. Bruno and Elmer, discussing strategy, looked up questioningly.

"Bruno," roared Wilbur, "Wizzle's got to go!"

Bruno smiled. "Sit down. We're having a committee meeting. Welcome to Operation Quake."

* * *

Mr. Wizzle went to bed that night in a state of nervous tension. He had placed a crystal glass carefully on the night table beside his bed and stood a spoon up in the glass. If there was another tremor, this would be his early warning.

As he climbed into bed, the spoon rattled sharply in the glass. He looked around nervously, trying to calm the beating of his heart. This would never do. He had to be sensible.

He lay down on his back, closed his eyes and opened them again, noticing that the ceiling light fixture was right over the bed. If it came down, it would kill him. He got up, causing the spoon and glass to rattle again, and pushed the bed all the way up against the far wall, under the window. That was a good idea — an emergency exit. Come on, get a grip on things, he told himself. He climbed back into bed and, after much tossing and turning, finally fell asleep.

Mr. Wizzle awoke early, with a start, the bright sun from the window shining in his eyes. He yawned, stretched and got up. "Wonderful! What a wonderful morning!" he declared aloud, even though his head was pounding from insufficient sleep. Sturgeon had been right. There was no earthquake fault. He'd probably imagined it all. What a relief! He felt so invigorated that he began to do deep knee bends. The spoon in the glass vibrated from his movements, and he laughed at his anxiety of the previous night.

He went out to the linen closet, grabbed a towel for his shower and re-entered the bedroom. The spoon was still rattling in the glass. The fixture was swaying from side to side and the floor began to vibrate under his feet. Then came the roar, louder this time, and he could feel a deep churning in his stomach.

"Earthquake!"

* * *

"There," said Bruno. "Switch it off. I think he's had enough for this morning."

Wilbur had a look of wonder on his face. "And that's honestly making an earthquake in his house?"

Elmer nodded.

Boots stirred in his bed and looked up sleepily. "What's going on at this hour of the morning? Wilbur? Elmer? Where did you guys come from? Bruno, what's going on? You never get up before a quarter to nine."

"I changed my hours," said Bruno, "when I changed my colleagues."

Bruno, Elmer and Wilbur sat at a corner table in the dining hall at lunch that day, listening to an earnest Chris Talbot.

"Then he said that he and his software had decided that

I was much too artistic ever to become a well-rounded person. So I pointed out that maybe I didn't want to be a well-rounded person and he gave me five demerits for mouthing off. He confiscated all my art supplies and switched me out of my art courses into physics, chemistry and algebraic structures. Now my average is going to go down twenty percent, not to mention that I hate that kind of stuff."

"That's a real bummer," said Bruno sympathetically. "What do you think you can do about it?"

"I want to join your committee," said Chris positively. "You were right all along, Bruno. We've got to get rid of Wizzle."

"We're well on the way already," said Bruno cheerfully. "Elmer, tell the man about Operation Quake."

* * *

Mr. Wizzle leaned back. "Now, Rampulsky, I have something very interesting planned for you."

Sidney squirmed in his chair, tipping himself over sideways. "Sorry, sir." He scrambled to his feet and sat down again.

"You've illustrated our point exactly," said Mr. Wizzle. "You're far too clumsy. You need something that will teach you grace and coordination. By special arrangement with Miss Peabody, you will be joining the beginners' ballet class at Scrimmage's."

Sidney leapt to his feet, banging his knee against the desk. "Ow! But sir —"

"No buts, Rampulsky. With your every motion you more than prove the need for this project. Their course convenes at three o'clock, so you will be dismissed five minutes early from your last class of the afternoon, starting today."

"But — but sir, you can't *do* this to me! I'll be the only guy there and —"

"This is your prescribed course of study, Rampulsky, arrived at through great effort and expense. Don't argue with me."

"But I can't just go over there and —"

"That will do," said Mr. Wizzle firmly. "Presuming to argue with me will cost you five demerits."

"I won't go!" howled Sidney.

"Ten demerits."

"I'll go," mumbled Sidney.

"Fine," said Mr. Wizzle. "And I want to see two hundred lines — *I will obey fully all the rules of Macdonald Hall.* You may go. Send Anderson in, will you?"

Sidney left and Pete Anderson entered the office.

"You wanted to see me, Mr. Wizzle, sir?" he said meekly.

"Yes, Anderson. Sit down. I'd like to have you write a few more tests."

Pete turned deathly white. "More tests? Like the real hard one we had to write the first day?"

"They're not hard, Anderson. They're opinion tests."

"Gee," said Pete, "I must have really flunked that first one!"

"No one fails, Anderson. Your results were just a little puzzling, that's all. The software needs some more data."

"Mr. Wizzle, do you think you could give me some books so I can study before I write those tests?"

"There's nothing to study," said Mr. Wizzle, a trifle impatiently. "It's just your own opinions."

Pete's brow furrowed. "What if my own opinions are the wrong answers?"

"Anderson, are you being deliberately dense?"

"Sir?"

"Oh, all right. Never mind. Report to me for testing at three o'clock every day this week. Dismissed."

* * *

Sidney Rampulsky, dressed in his Macdonald Hall phys. ed. uniform, stood in the middle of Miss Scrimmage's gym. The ballet class was taking place in one half of the room; the other half was being used for advanced gymnastics.

"Okay, Sidney," sang out Miss Smedley, "now don't be self-conscious. Go ahead and try the steps."

She put on the music and Sidney started, concentrating hard on his feet. He was determined to get it right this time so he wouldn't have to come back. He began to dance sideways as directed.

"That's far enough, Sidney," called Miss Smedley. Then, more urgently, "That's far enough, Sidney! Sidney!"

His intense concentration blocking her warning, Sidney kept on dancing, tripping across a bench at the sidelines, knocking it over and sending four girls sprawling. He got up and continued to follow the steps as he had learned them.

"That's it, Sidney. Very good. Nice and easy does it, Sidney. Sidney! Look out for the wall! *Look out for the wall.*"

Still concentrating, Sidney bounced off the wall, dislodging the chalk board. It crashed to the floor, the slate shattering into little pieces. A cloud of chalk dust rose.

"Okay, Sidney, stop," called Miss Smedley, choking in the dust. "That's enough, Sidney. Sidney! You're going to the wrong side of the gym! Sydney! *Stop!*"

Still mentally following his steps, Sidney danced into the midst of the gymnastics class, bumping into the balance beam and knocking it over. There was an enormous crash as the beam hit the polished floor and a girl went flying.

"*No, Sidney!*" Miss Smedley was screaming now. "*Please! No! Stop! Oh, I can't look — !*"

Sidney ricocheted off the far wall and bumped into the uneven bars. The girl who was performing on them screamed as she and the bars fell heavily to the floor.

Still following his routine, and oblivious of all pleading and screaming, Sidney danced on. He wandered aimlessly between the parallel bars, causing the shocked gymnast working on them to leap for her life.

"*Stop, Sidney!*" In desperation, Miss Smedley switched off the music, scratching the record from start to finish, but Sidney was no longer aware of what was going on around him. He had been sent here to dance, and he was dancing. He spun around twice and jumped up, landing right on the springboard for the vaulting horse. He sailed through the air, hitting the horse at an angle and knocking it over with a drop kick. It crashed to the floor and broke into three pieces. Then he began the running start for his grand finale.

Amid tumultuous cheers from the girls, who had crowded to the other side of the room and were watching in awe, Sidney pirouetted across the gym, stubbing his toe on the mat by the climbing apparatus. Desperately he snatched at air and finally gripped a loose climbing rope. With a terrified howl, he swung through the air feet first and became hopelessly entangled in a rope ladder, hanging upside-down in the climbing apparatus.

"Uh — I'm finished, Miss Smedley," he called, "but I don't think I know how to get down."

Miss Scrimmage's girls broke into loud applause and cheering, and ran for the climber to aid the suspended Sidney.

"Girls, don't!" cried Miss Smedley in horror, watching as they all began to ascend. "You can't all be on the climber at the same time! The weight —"

There was an awful cracking sound as the frame of the apparatus slowly gave way. The whole set-up — Sidney, girls and all — fell with a tremendous crash to the floor.

The gym door burst open and in rushed Miss Peabody. She spied Sidney amid the debris and made straight for him.

"A little clumsy?! A *little* clumsy?!" she shouted, hauling him bodily out of the wreckage. "I'll give Wizzle a little clumsy!"

She grabbed Sidney by the scruff of the neck and the seat of the pants and began to run him out the door. "Stop crying!" she tossed over her shoulder at the whimpering Miss Smedley. Pushing Sidney, the Assistant Headmistress burst out the front door of the school, propelled him to the highway, saw there was no traffic, and hurled him out into the road. "Now, *beat it!* And don't come back!"

Sidney ran for his life. Only one thing could save him now — Bruno's committee.

Chapter 8

the committee

"Miss Scrimmage, would you kindly repeat that?" said Mr. Sturgeon into the telephone that afternoon. "One of my boys destroyed your gymnasium? Miss Scrimmage, I hardly see how that's possible. The boys were all in classes . . . Mr. Wizzle sent him?" The Headmaster's grip tightened on the pen he was holding. "Did he? I see. Tell me, Miss Scrimmage, would the boy's name by any chance be Rampulsky? . . . I thought so . . . *Twelve hundred dollars damage?.* . . But how? . . . No, Miss Scrimmage, I don't really want to know. I shall look into the matter. Good afternoon."

Mr. Sturgeon hung up the phone and walked to the outer office where Mr. Wizzle was pounding a keyboard.

"Wizzle, "said the Headmaster gravely, "what's all this about Sidney Rampulsky taking ballet lessons at Scrimmage's?"

Mr. Wizzle turned around. "Oh, that. Well, it seems that Rampulsky had — uh — a little accident and — "

"A *little* accident? Would you call twelve hundred dollars damage a little accident?"

"Well, he had an accident, and now Miss Peabody's a little upset." He grimaced. On the phone earlier she had bluntly threatened to come over and take the twelve hundred dollars out of his hide.

"Have you informed the Board about this?" asked Mr. Sturgeon.

"Well, no. I mean, I was just about to and — uh — er — I'll do it right now."

"Good," approved Mr. Sturgeon. "And make sure you tell them exactly what happened, without leaving anything out."

Mr. Wizzle watched as his WizzleWare automatically switched to screen-saver mode and the printer whirred into action. What with the earthquakes and now this, things seemed to have taken a turn for the worse.

Mr. Sturgeon returned to his office and sat down with a frown. He would certainly not have a moment's peace as long as Wizzle was here.

* * *

"Oh, man!" Pete Anderson was holding his head at dinner that evening. "Those tests — were they ever hard! There's no way I passed! The best I could have done was about thirty percent — forty, tops! And Wizzle's got more for me to do every day! I'm doomed!"

Bruno, surrounded by Wilbur, Chris and Elmer, chewed thoughtfully. "What are you going to do about it?"

"Well," said Pete, "I thought maybe — you know, maybe I — that is, we — uh — do you still have your committee?"

"Forget the tests," grinned Bruno. "Welcome back."

A loud crash signified that Sidney was at the table. "Bruno," he said, picking up the cutlery that had fallen from his tray, "the most terrible thing just happened to me!" He related the events of his first ballet lesson, which had the boys howling with laughter.

"Then Miss Peabody threw me across the road. It's not funny, you guys! I want to join your committee and get rid of Wizzle before he finds me and gives me demerits!"

Larry Wilson and Mark Davies sat down at the end of the table. "I don't know what you guys are talking about," said Mark, "but if it's getting rid of Wizzle, I'm in. He just kicked me out of being editor of the school newspaper!"

"Yeah?" said Wilbur between bites. "So who's the editor now?"

"Pete," said Mark sourly.

Pete choked on his sandwich. "Me? Editor?"

"Yeah. The results of your latest tests are just in, and Wizzle says you need the job more than I do."

"Oh, no," moaned Pete. "Now I have to do the newspaper! I was better off with the tests!"

"How about you, Larry?" asked Bruno. "Are you joining up with us?"

"Sure," said Larry.

"What's your grievance?" asked Chris.

"I don't have one," replied Larry. "I just like being on committees."

Bruno stood up at the end of the table, smiling hugely. "This is fantastic! The whole organization's here!"

"What about Boots?" called someone.

Bruno flushed momentarily. "Boots has a few personal problems to work out." The triumphant expression returned to his face. "But we're a committee again. We can *fight* again!" Dramatically, he ripped off his tie and threw it to the floor.

"Bruno Walton, what was the purpose of that outburst?"

Everyone wheeled to see Mr. Wizzle standing in the doorway, writing in his notebook.

"Five demerits. And put your tie back on. Now, Anderson, I have some good news for you. Come to my office for a moment."

"See you around, editor," said Bruno, knotting his tie.

Pete tossed him a worried glance and followed Mr. Wizzle.

* * *

It was two o'clock in the morning, but there was still vigorous activity in Miss Scrimmage's apple orchard. The Blue Squadron, led by Cathy Burton and Diane Grant, marched in formation up and down between the rows of trees. They had been drilling every night, in addition to normal practice time, and were easily the most expert squadron of the four.

Cathy marched at the head of the troops, carrying the flagpole that held the bright blue banner. She turned around. "Company, halt!" she whispered loudly. "Okay, we're definitely going to win the big parade tomorrow. That twenty-four-hour pass is as good as ours."

There was restrained cheering.

"Everyone get a good night's sleep, and tomorrow morning wake up bright and chipper and ready to march your little guts out. Anybody who fouls up dies."

The girls all trooped back to their rooms.

"You know, "whispered Diane as she and Cathy crept into the residence, "your little pep talk back there sounded a lot like Peabody."

Cathy cast her a withering glare. "If you want to be my friend, don't say things like that."

* * *

About the same time, the door of the Macdonald Hall guest cottage burst open and Mr. Wizzle raced out into the night. Barefoot, he ran about twenty metres and hurled himself face first onto the ground, where he lay panting.

Cautiously he looked up. The campus was dark. No one else had noticed the earthquake. He touched the ground. It seemed to be over.

He got to his feet and began to walk slowly back to his house. The upstairs light went on in the Headmaster's cottage and Mr. Sturgeon's head appeared at the window.

"I say, Wizzle," he called down. "Any problem?"

"Oh, no. No, "replied Mr. Wizzle with a heartiness he was far from feeling. "I was just — taking a little walk. You know — to get some air."

"I would not presume to lecture," said the Headmaster, "but might I point out that you are in your underwear?"

"Oh, well — uh — ha, ha — we're all boys here."

"Yes," agreed Mr. Sturgeon, "except perhaps my wife and the three hundred or so young girls across the road. In your future walks, Wizzle, kindly be more circumspect in your choice of costume. Good night."

Mr. Wizzle fled back home.

The Headmaster shut the window. "Mildred, I think Wizzle's cracking up. He was running around out there in his underwear."

"You must be mistaken, dear. Mr. Wizzle would never do such a thing."

"Mildred, would I lie to you?"

"Oh, go to sleep, William."

* * *

The boys sat at their usual table at lunch on Saturday discussing strategy.

"Okay," said Bruno, "today's the big membership drive. Today we're going to go out there and recruit all the guys to help us on the committee. Get them to join up, and tell them to come to our mammoth rally tonight."

"What mammoth rally?" asked Wilbur suspiciously.

"Our big anti-Wizzle meeting. We're all going to get together and get organized — you know, set up subcommittees and departments. We're going to be more efficient than WizzleWare."

"Actually," began Elmer, "a cutting-edge software program — "

"Stow it, Elm," said Bruno. "We'll all have to work really hard recruiting people. I want ten choice guys from each of you. Including us, that'll make around ninety."

"Around *ninety*?"

"We can get more if we need them," said Bruno.

"Where can we meet that'll accommodate ninety people?" asked Chris, who was of a practical turn of mind.

"In the woods out back," replied Bruno.

"Count me out," said everybody.

"You guys all tried to quit once before," Bruno reminded them, "and look where you are now."

"Okay," muttered Wilbur between bites. "But just in case, I'm going to enjoy my last two meals. If we're caught — "

"Don't worry," grinned Bruno. "I never get caught."

* * *

The girls of the Blue Squadron were due to parade last. They lined up, clad in dress tunics with blue arm bands, waiting for the White team to finish marching.

"We're a cinch!" crowed Cathy to Diane. "Did you see how lousy the other squads were? We're going to win this parade by a landslide, and then it's bye-bye Peabody for a whole day!"

"Okay!" bellowed Miss Peabody's voice from the reviewing platform. "Blue Squadron!"

Cathy picked up her flag and took her place at the front of her troops. "Company, march!"

They started off marching in perfect formation, moving as one person. All those practice hours were worth it, thought Cathy in jubilation. They were picture-perfect. Even Miss Peabody had to be impressed. She felt like singing, but one didn't sing while one marched.

"Eyes right!" commanded Cathy. She dipped the flag in front of the reviewing stand, but she dipped it too low and the tip of the pole stubbed into the ground and stuck there. Cathy marched forward into the flag and bounced back, knocking over Diane, who fell backward into the rank behind her. Rank by rank, the entire Blue Squadron marching team keeled over backward like a row of bowling pins.

Overcome by guilt, humiliation and the pain of losing, Cathy scrambled to her feet, ripped the flagpole from the ground and screamed something decidedly unladylike.

"Catherine!" Miss Scrimmage covered her ears and closed her eyes.

Cathy hefted the pole like a javelin, reared back in rage and hurled it into the apple orchard.

"Blue Squadron," barked Miss Peabody, "get off the field! Red Squadron, you're the winners. Congratulations."

The girls on the red team went into raptures of celebration.

"Burton, front and centre!"

* * *

Miss Peabody leaned back in her office chair. "Cooled off yet, Burton?"

"Yes, Miss Peabody," said Cathy, still shaking with rage.

"That was a pretty nice parade you had there. I can see you put a lot of work into it."

Cathy looked up in surprise.

"As for what happened — well, things like that are always going to happen, even in the Marines."

Cathy looked at her strangely. Could this be Peabody's version of kindness?

"Yes, it was pretty good there for a while," said Miss Peabody. "Too bad you had to open up your big mouth and ruin it. That was stupid. Miss Scrimmage wants you punished for foul language." She grinned. "Run a couple of laps this afternoon — if you have time."

"Yes, Miss Peabody," said Cathy, mystified.

"Right!" barked Miss Peabody, the smile gone. "Now, push off. I have work to do."

Cathy left, frowning in perplexity. Had she been punished or what?

* * *

Boots O'Neal walked into the outer office of the Faculty Building bearing a message for Mr. Wizzle from Coach Flynn. Mrs. Davis was not at her desk and Mr. Wizzle's office was empty, so he stepped towards Mr. Sturgeon's oak door, which was ajar. Inside he could hear the Headmaster talking with Mr. Wizzle. Although the conversation was muffled, he could distinctly make out Mr. Wizzle mentioning something that was uppermost in Boots's mind: Bruno Walton.

He did not mean to eavesdrop, but nevertheless he stood rooted to the spot.

"Bruno Walton is at the root of every problem we've ever had," Mr. Wizzle was saying. "His behaviour is atrocious; he's disrespectful and rebellious. Why, I'm sure he was responsible for that *Macdonald Hall Free Press.* The minute I mentioned it at the assembly, every eye went to him. And the boy obviously does not take his education seriously. Just look at the results of his tests. In question nine on this one he says he prefers possessions to friends; in question fourteen, he holds friendship more valuable than worldly goods. Or this one — he answered (a) for every question. And in the third test, he simply filled in everything. My software suffered a small breakdown trying to analyze his scan sheet."

Mr. Sturgeon stifled a smile. "I'll have a word with the boy."

"And yesterday," Mr. Wizzle went on, undeterred, "he handed in the last of his lines — three hundred and fifty of them. Three hundred and forty-nine were in order, but one of them, buried in the middle, read — and I quote — 'I will not rest until I kick this turkey out of Macdonald Hall'! Can you imagine that?"

"I see, "said the Headmaster, his expression inscrutable.

"I'm giving Walton five demerits for not taking the testing seriously, and five more for writing that insulting line. That gives him fifty-six. I recommend that he be expelled at once."

Outside the door, Boots felt his heart skip a beat. "Recommendation considered and rejected," said Mr. Sturgeon immediately.

"Perhaps you didn't quite understand me," said Mr. Wizzle. "Bruno Walton is a troublemaker."

"I understood you perfectly," said the Headmaster. "The subject is closed."

"But Mr. Sturgeon, according to the Wizzle System — "

"The Wizzle System is mistaken," said Mr. Sturgeon coldly.

"Well, I don't like to say this, sir, but the Board has given me considerable authority here."

"Not over my boys," said Mr. Sturgeon firmly.

Mr. Wizzle sighed. "Very well, sir. We'll try it your way. But I firmly believe that Bruno Walton is a bad influence at Macdonald Hall."

"Your opinion has been noted."

* * *

Bruno lay on his bed contemplating his committee and mentally planning tonight's meeting. There was a tremendous crash and the door flew open, the lock broken. In hopped Boots, cradling his left foot tenderly.

"Bruno, I've got to talk to you!"

Bruno looked at him questioningly. "What is it?"

"Yeah, uh — " Boots paused. Should Bruno be told how close he'd come to being expelled? No. The Fish had stuck up for him this time. But how long would that last? "Uh — what's new?"

"Nothing that would interest you," said Bruno, "so if you're finished, I've got a lot to do."

Oh, no! thought Boots. If he didn't keep an eye on Bruno, his roommate could be expelled! Despite everything he had to keep his friend out of trouble.

"I — I want to join your committee." Boots regretted the words as soon as they were out of his mouth. This would only encourage Bruno to make more trouble!

Without saying a word Bruno got up off his bed and began to remove the masking tape that divided the room. An enormous grin split his face. "About ninety of us are meeting tonight."

Boots smiled grudgingly. As a committee member, maybe he could maintain some control over his roommate.

* * *

Illuminated by moonlight, Bruno Walton stood up before the crowd of boys in the woods behind Macdonald Hall. Most of them had come against their better judgment. They were looking around nervously, asking each other if they knew the reason behind this secret meeting.

"The meeting will come to order," said Bruno. Then, less formally, "Hi, guys. Glad you could make it."

"What is this?" piped someone.

"This," announced Bruno grandly, "is The Committee."

"What committee?"

Bruno looked at them solemnly. "*The* Committee."

"The Committee?"

"*The* Committee?"

"We'll all be expelled. I'm leaving."

There was general agreement, and some of the boys began to walk away.

"Wait!" pleaded Elmer.

"Hear us out, at least," said Bruno. "If you don't hear us out, we'll all get mad. Have any of you ever seen Wilbur when he's mad?"

"Okay, Bruno," called someone impatiently, "let's hear it."

"The purpose of The Committee is to get rid of Wizzle," began Bruno, "and —"

"Well, why didn't you say so?" Instantly, the crowd was on Bruno's side.

"I can't stand that guy Wizzle!"

"He gave me so many demerits that I had to write lines!"

"He gave me so many lines I got demerits for not writing them!"

"I can never remember how to tie my tie. Should the little end be longer than the big end?"

"Wizzle confiscated my rock collection because it wasn't making efficient use of space."

"When no one was looking, I kicked his computer."

"Good for you."

"Okay," said Bruno. "To signify that you're with The Committee, I want you all to come up here and press this remote control button. It makes an earthquake at Wizzle's house, so it's kind of your initiation into the organization."

One by one, the boys went up to Elmer's remote control button and pressed it.

"Now," said Bruno, "let me tell you about Operation Shut-Up."

Boots looked at him. "Operation Shut-Up?"

"Wouldn't it be great if Wizzle couldn't say anything?"

"Sure," said Boots. "But how are we going to shut him up?"

"We're not," grinned Bruno. "We're going to do the next best thing. We're going to shut up his WizzleWare. Okay, listen carefully, guys . . . "

Chapter 9

the paper chase

On Monday morning Mr. Wizzle had dark circles under his eyes. The earthquakes were getting worse. On Saturday night he could have sworn there had been a hundred little tremors, followed on Sunday night by a quake even bigger than before. On both nights he had been forced to abandon his cottage. After all, who knew just when the entire fault line might cave in completely? He winced. Every time he left the house in a big hurry, there was Mr. Sturgeon at his window. The man was getting to be a regular peeping Tom!

Mr. Wizzle suppressed a yawn. He'd been planning to analyze the teacher efficiency reports he'd been putting together. It was just a matter of printing them.

A flashing red light on the print console drew his eye. "Out of paper," said Wizzle aloud. How strange! He was certain he had loaded the tray only Friday. He glanced at the spare box on the floor. Empty. This was impossible. It had been full on Friday afternoon! He went down the hall, took out his master key and unlocked the supply room door. He walked in and opened up a new box of inkjet paper. There inside the carton sat twelve rolls of toilet paper. He opened another box: more toilet paper. And another. All the boxes were filled with toilet paper. Furious, he opened a carton marked *Toilet Paper*. Well, that at least was correct.

Mr. Wizzle stormed to his office telephone and dialled the number of Systems Supply Ltd., the office outlet he dealt with.

"This is Walter C. Wizzle at Macdonald Hall . . . Not Wuzzle, Wizzle . . . Listen, where is my inkjet paper? . . . Yes, I know the order has been completed. You sent me toilet paper . . . What do you mean, you don't handle toilet paper? You handled ten boxes in my direction . . . Yes, while you're looking into it, get me a rush order for another ten boxes. And make sure it's inkjet paper this time, will you? I have a great deal of reports to print . . . Yes, I guess noon will be soon enough. Thank you."

Standing outside the door, Larry Wilson, office messenger and committee member, smiled to himself. Operation Shut-Up had sidelined Mr. Wizzle at least until noon. And now that they knew a truck was coming . . .

At 12:05 the truck from Systems Supply Ltd. pulled up in front of the Faculty Building. Chris Talbot rushed out to meet it.

"Hi," he said. "Inkjet paper? Great. Just drop it off at that building there — yeah, the sign says Dormitory 3. They're waiting for you."

The truck moved along to Dormitory 3 and delivered Mr. Wizzle's printer paper into the eager hands of Bruno, Boots and Wilbur. With a flourish Bruno signed the delivery ticket and the driver left.

"You didn't sign Mr. Wizzle's name, did you?" asked Boots nervously as the three boys began to stack the paper up against the wall of room 306, along with the paper they had taken earlier from the stock room.

"Of course not," said Bruno. "I signed *G. Gavin Gunhold*. He's the shipper-receiver around here."

"That's the last of them," said Wilbur. "Let's go eat lunch."

At two o'clock Walter C. Wizzle was on the phone again. "Hello, This is Wizzle again . . . No, not Wuzzle, Wizzle! . . . I'm calling about those ten boxes of computer paper you promised would be here by noon. Where are they? . . . You can't have a signed delivery slip, because I never got the delivery . . . G. Gavin Gunhold? There is no G. Gavin Gunhold here! You delivered my paper to the wrong place! . . . All right, look into it. But in the meantime ship me ten more boxes as soon as possible . . . All right, four o'clock is fine."

Okay, thought Larry Wilson outside the door, four o'clock is fine.

The Systems Supply Ltd. truck came driving up the highway just after 4 PM. It was about a kilometre from the school when Mark Davies stepped out into its path, waving frantically. The truck pulled over onto the soft shoulder and the driver got out.

"Excuse me, sir," said Mark, "but have you got a monkey wrench I can borrow? There's something wrong with my bicycle." Actually, it was Coach Flynn's bicycle, and Bruno and Boots had taken off the front wheel.

"Sure thing. I've got a whole tool box. Maybe I can give you a hand."

As he laboured with Mark over the dismantled bike, he failed to see Bruno, Boots and a Committee Task Force removing ten cartons from the back of the truck and replacing them with ten of their own. By the time Flynn's wheel was back on, the switch was complete and everyone was hidden away.

Mr. Wizzle eagerly opened up one of the cartons that had just arrived.

"Toilet paper! They did it again!" In a rage, he rushed to the telephone. "Hello, this is Wizzle . . . No, not Wuzzle, Wizzle! . . . I just received my order and you gave me toilet paper again! . . . Yes, I know you don't sell it, but that's what you sent me! Have you people gone crazy? . . . Well, I want some of the right paper now. I will personally drive over there and pick it up . . . What do you mean you're all out of inkjet paper? . . . Yes, I know some guy ordered twenty boxes just today! But I never got a single sheet of it! . . . All right, all right, all right! I'll call back tomorrow. Do what you can for me, will you? Good-bye." He hung up emphatically. Now that was just peachy! No paper!

* * *

"The parade was just the beginning," announced Miss Peabody at the assembly. "You girls still need some excitement and exertion. You need to experience the thrill of dropping into bed at night feeling completely fatigued.

You need the exhilaration of competition!"

An uneasy murmur ran through the gym. Miss Scrimmage shifted uncomfortably in her chair.

In the seventh row, Cathy and Diane looked at each other in desperation. Now what was Peabody up to?

"I've ordered three hundred water pistols and a whole load of food colouring," Miss Peabody went on with growing enthusiasm. "We're going to have war games."

Miss Scrimmage gave an audible gasp and reached in her purse for her smelling salts.

The girls stared at the Assistant Headmistress, mute with shock. Of all the things they had been sent to finishing school for, war games were the last on the list.

"My goodness!" blurted Miss Scrimmage in a high state of nerves. "Water pistols! Food colouring! War games! It all seems so — unladylike!"

"That's right!" exclaimed Miss Peabody. "It isn't ladylike — it's war! And it develops vital skills like speed, agility and strategic planning-skills these girls will need someday — all in a spirit of healthy competition. Blue and White Squadrons against Red and Green Squadrons, fighting with harmless weapons to occupy the orchard. We'll put some backbone into these jellyfish! And by the way, the winning army gets a weekend trip with Miss Scrimmage."

"A whole weekend!" whispered Cathy. "Forty-eight hours without Peabody! This we win!"

"That's what you said last time," Diane whispered back.

"Shhh. I'm planning strategy."

* * *

Coming from the Faculty Building, Bruno Walton walked directly to Dormitory 1. Now he had fifty-six demerits and four hundred lines. This was a job for The Committee's Lines Department. He approached the door of room 114 and gave the secret knock.

"Lines Department," came Mark Davies' voice. "How may we help you?"

The door swung open and Bruno was treated to the sight of efficiency at its best. The room was full of boys seated at desks and tables, industriously writing lines.

Bruno whistled in admiration. He filled out:

NAME: *Bruno Walton*

POSITION IN THE COMMITTEE: *President*

NUMBER OF LINES: *400*

SAMPLE OF HANDWRITING: *Wizzle must go!* (Bruno scrawled this in his usual unintelligible hand.)

PICK-UP DATE: *Friday Morning*

"Gee," said Mark, "that's pretty soon for all those lines. But we'll see what we can do." He placed Bruno's application on a stack of many others. "We're really busy here."

"You're doing a great job," said Bruno. "See you."

* * *

Mr. Sturgeon walked into his kitchen and looked around hopefully. "Where's dinner, Mildred? Haven't you started it yet?"

"It's all ready, dear. It's in the refrigerator."

"Well, hadn't you better heat it up?"

"No, it's a cold dinner. We're having a big salad and some other vegetable dishes."

The Headmaster's face fell. "Oh, no. You've invited Wizzle. How many times do I have to tell you how much I dislike that young man?"

"Oh, William! You're Headmaster and you have social

responsibilities. I've also invited Miss Scrimmage and Miss Peabody."

Mr. Sturgeon groaned. "Your timing is off, Mildred. You should invite Miss Peabody when you're serving raw meat."

"Now that's enough, William," said his wife sternly. "This time I want you to be genuinely sociable. Your attitude toward others leaves a great deal to be desired."

"I'm sure Wizzle's going crazy," said Mr. Sturgeon, helping himself to a piece of leftover cold chicken. "He spent all day today on the phone raving about toilet paper. And I've told you about how he's taken to running out of his house in his underwear in the middle of the night."

"You're exaggerating, William. Mr. Wizzle is really a very nice young man." She glared. "I wish you wouldn't lean on the counter and munch like that. You'll spoil your dinner."

"My dinner is already spoiled," replied her husband grimly. "Wizzle is going to be here."

The doorbell rang. Mr. and Mrs. Sturgeon went together to answer it and found all three guests there. The company settled themselves in the living room and engaged in polite conversation. Mrs. Sturgeon was definitely on her guard, skillfully leading the chitchat away from controversial topics and coaxing her husband into taking part.

Dinner was a pleasant affair, with Mrs. Sturgeon continuing in her role as the perfect hostess, and topics like the weather being discussed at great length. Finally coffee was served.

Mr. Wizzle leaned back in his chair. "So, Miss Peabody, you still haven't taken me up on my invitation to come over and have a look at my WizzleWare."

"That's right," said Miss Peabody. "I've got better things to do than spend my time looking at a bunch of computers."

Mr. Wizzle chuckled gently. "WizzleWare isn't computers, Miss Peabody. It's a way that computers can work. A state-of-the-art software system provides invaluable assistance to a school and, of course, is a major investment."

"All right, I'll rephrase that," said Miss Peabody. "It's an *expensive* computer. Anyway, it's no match for good, solid administration. At our school I'm really starting to see some results in the toughening up of those girls. Here, with that fancy system of yours, you're breeding a bunch of paunchy flabs just like yourself."

Mr. Wizzle stiffened. "Are you insinuating that my philosophy of education does not build physical strength and character?"

"I didn't insinuate anything," said Miss Peabody. "I said it right out."

"More coffee, anyone?" asked Mrs. Sturgeon anxiously.

"I'm sure there are wonderful merits to both systems," put in Miss Scrimmage weakly.

"The girls are up at six-thirty every morning doing calisthenics," boasted Miss Peabody.

"Even in bad weather," added Miss Scrimmage woefully.

"Yes, well, I'd like to see the Macdonald Hall boys do that," said Miss Peabody. "And I'd like to see a software program do a jumping jack!"

"I'll give the matter serious consideration," said Mr. Wizzle thoughtfully. "Heavy exercise might channel some of their — uh — mischievous tendencies."

Miss Peabody grinned. "You've got a discipline problem, huh, Wizzle? I'll bet your biggest problem is the greatest kid in the school."

Mr. Sturgeon smiled and thought of Bruno Walton.

"At Scrimmage's we've got this girl named Burton. What a girl! What spirit! What character! She spends half her time running punishment laps, of course, but that just brings out more of the spirit."

"It also brings out more offensive words," said Miss Scrimmage primly.

"Wait till the war games," promised Miss Peabody. "You'll see what strong stuff Burton is made of."

Mr. Sturgeon sat bolt upright. "Uh — I beg your pardon, Miss Peabody? You did say war games?"

"Right! Our girls are having war games. The exhilaration and exertion will be good for them. And the strategy planning will sharpen their wits."

There was dead silence, and then: "Would anyone like a little dessert?"

* * *

Bruno stretched out on his bed. "What a great day! The Committee is working out perfectly! In no time at all Wizzle will be packed and gone."

Boots looked worried. "I don't know, Bruno." He frowned at the twenty-nine boxes of computer paper stacked in the room. "What if something goes wrong?"

Bruno shrugged. "What could possibly go wrong? The Committee is set up tight as a drum."

There was a tapping at the window. Bruno and Boots raised the blind to reveal Larry Wilson skulking in the bushes.

110

"Oh, hi, Larry. What's up?"

"Surprise dorm inspection," Larry hissed. "You guys better hide that paper!"

Boots went white to the ears. "We can't hide it! How can we hide it? There's no place to hide it! Where can we hide it?"

Bruno closed the window. "Hmmm," he said thoughtfully.

"Don't just stand there!" babbled Boots. "Do something! We've got to do something! We're going to be expelled!"

"This is a job for Committee Security," said Bruno determinedly. "They'll be here. We haven't got a thing to worry about. See? There's Wilbur now with the signal."

Boots watched as Wilbur walked to a central point visible to all three dormitories, took out a huge white handkerchief and blew his nose mightily.

In seconds shadowy figures began to appear from all directions as the Security Department's Emergency Task Force swung into action. After a short briefing they formed a human chain, starting outside the window of room 306. As Bruno and Boots handed out the boxes of printer paper, they were passed down the chain and into a room in Dormitory 2. Just as Boots handed the last box out the window, there was a sharp knock at the door.

"Dormitory inspection!" The pass key was in the lock.

Bruno slammed the window shut. "Coming, Mr. Wizzle, sir."

Mr. Wizzle and Mr. Sturgeon entered the room.

"Ah — not ready for bed yet — two demerits. Room very messy — another two demerits. Kind of dusty. Do clean it up." He took out his notebook and began to scribble. "All,

Bruno Walton. That gives you sixty demerits. Four hundred and fifty lines."

"But sir," protested Bruno, "you just assigned me four hundred."

"Yes, and you deserved every one of them. Okay, that's all."

Bruno and Boots cast a beseeching look at their Headmaster.

Mr. Sturgeon nodded at them. "Carry on, Walton — O' Neal."

The door closed behind them. The inspection was over.

"The nerve of that Wizzle!" ranted Bruno. "The Lines Department's going to kill me!"

"The Lines Department!" exclaimed Boots in horror. "They've got five rooms in Dormitory 1 full of tables and chairs! What if Wizzle and The Fish walk in on that?"

"Don't worry," soothed Bruno. "Security has Task Force B over there. They'll look after things." He pounded a fist on the desk. "I just can't stand these sneak inspections! Tonight Wizzle gets another earthquake — at four o'clock in the morning!"

There was a knock on the window. It was Task Force A bringing back the inkjet paper.

Chapter 10

war!

On Tuesday afternoon Mr. Wizzle drove his old white Toyota, packed full to the roof with cartons of printer paper, into the driveway of Macdonald Hall. He stopped right in front of the Faculty Building, got out and opened the trunk.

Bruno Walton watched through the glass doors from the outer office. "Okay, Larry, start!"

Larry dialled Miss Scrimmage's number. "Hello, may I please speak with Miss Peabody? Yes, thank you. Tell her Mr. Wizzle is waiting on the line." Larry switched on the outdoor intercom. "Mr. Wizzle, telephone, please. Mr. Wizzle."

Bruno dashed out the side exit. In through the front

door marched Mr. Wizzle.

"Miss Peabody on line one, sir," said Larry.

"Thanks. I'll take it in my office."

As soon as Mr. Wizzle's office door closed, a Committee Task Force led by Bruno Walton fell on the car.

"Hello, Miss Peabody. Walter Wizzle speaking. What can I do for you? . . . Pardon me? . . . Well, no, I don't want anything. You called me . . . What do you mean you didn't? . . . Now please don't be abusive. I'm sure there's a rational explanation, Miss Peabody . . . Miss Peabody? . . . " He hung up. There was definitely something peculiar about that woman.

He went back out to his car and, with the assistance of some passing students, carried in the paper. With great relish he opened the first box with his pocket knife.

"Found your paper at last, eh, Wizzle?" said Mr. Sturgeon, passing by.

Mr. Wizzle smiled. "I've got a lot of work to catch up on." He lifted the carton flap. Inside were carefully stacked rows of white serviettes. "Napkins!" he howled in anguish. "Table napkins! Why would they give me table napkins?"

Mr. Sturgeon peered politely into the box. "Perhaps they ran out of toilet paper."

* * *

"Why would you give him napkins?" asked Chris Talbot at dinner.

Bruno shrugged. "We ran out of toilet paper."

"Hey, Bruno," said Mark, "I don't like to seem ungrateful for all your work as President of The Committee, but we in the Lines Department have enough to do without you racking up lines like they're going out of style. We're

114

not wizards, you know. They all had tears in their eyes when I handed out your four hundred and fifty."

Bruno grinned. "Sorry. Hey, I really want to congratulate the Security Department. That was great work last night getting us through inspection."

"Thanks," mumbled Wilbur, his mouth full of meat loaf.

"Now, Chris, Elmer — listen. The Committee needs an emergency backup weapon in case Wizzle holds out to the end. We're going to prepare for the ultimate protest demonstration. Guys, can you design me a giant helium balloon that looks like Wizzle?"

"Are you out of your mind?" Boots interrupted.

"Nope," said Bruno cheerfully.

"How giant?" asked Chris suspiciously.

"Oh — maybe thirty feet high."

Chris looked at Elmer. "Can you do it?"

Elmer chewed thoughtfully on a celery stalk. "With the proper materials it shouldn't be too difficult. It would be just like an inflatable boat, except in the shape of a man."

"If you can build it," said Chris, "I can make it look like Wizzle. It may take time, though — I mean, a balloon that big."

"No hurry," said Bruno. "It's just something we should be working on."

Boots sat silently contemplating what he had just heard. Mr. Wizzle thought Bruno was a troublemaker. Mr. Wizzle didn't know the half of it!

* * *

"Well," said Ruth Sidwell, captain of White Squadron, "don't you think we can win the war games without cheating?"

"Sure we can," said Cathy, "but why take the chance? Besides, there's no such thing as cheating. This is war. Peabody even said so."

"I hear the Red and Green teams have some pretty strong stuff planned," put in Diane.

"Yeah, well, we're going to make them wish they'd never enlisted," said Cathy. "We're being given little water pistols to fire our blue dye at the enemy. Tonight Diane and I are going to sneak down to the storeroom and get some plastic bags. Then we'll have bombs. We can post people in trees, dig trenches and build earthworks for defence. By the time these war games are over, the world will be blue and the orchard will be ours!"

"Aren't you getting a little carried away with all this?" asked Ruth uneasily.

"Of course not," said Cathy. "And after we've won, it's bye-bye Peabody for forty-eight hours. How's *that* for strategic logic?"

* * *

Bruno and Boots were sitting at their desks doing their homework on Thursday afternoon when the door opened and Larry Wilson rushed in.

"Hey, guys, look what I've got!" He handed Bruno a typed letter with that day's date of arrival stamped on it. "Mrs. Davis was opening the mail and I just happened to see this. It's for Wizzle from some geologists: Ignatz, Sediman and Mortimer."

Bruno read the letter out loud:

Dear Mr. Wizzle,

    It was with a good deal of amusement
that we read of your fears. The Great

```
Lakes-St. Lawrence Lowlands fault line is
the most ridiculous thing we have ever heard
of: It does not even exist, and could not
possibly present a threat to your house.
Therefore, the consensus here is that your
chances of survival are good.
                    Yours sincerely,
                    Harlan Ignatz.
```

"What are you going to do?" asked Boots. "You can't keep Mr. Wizzle's letter. That's interfering with the mail."

"Oh, we'll give him back his letter," said Bruno, "but first we'll have to make a few minor changes. Somebody get Mark. We'll need the print shop to make it look real . . . "

* * *

Mr. Wizzle sat back in his office chair and read the letter:

```
Dear Mr. Wizzle,
     It was with a good deal of concern that
we read of your fears. The Great Lakes-St.
Lawrence Lowlands fault line is the most dan-
gerous thing we have ever heard of. It does
surely exist and could very likely present a
threat to your house. Therefore, the consen-
sus here is that your chances of survival are
50-50.
                    Yours sincerely,
                    Harlan Ignatz.
```

Mr. Wizzle jumped up and began to pace nervously. This was certainly disconcerting news, although he should have known it anyway. After all, he'd been having tremors every night lately. He sat down on the corner of his desk and wiped the sweat off his brow. He had nothing to worry about. He had perfected his escape and could be out his bedroom window to safety in four seconds flat. With practice, he could easily cut that down to three. Still, the whole thing was an unnecessary emotional strain on him.

A lot of things had been bothering him lately. Like the printer paper. He still didn't have any. It was as if an evil spirit were keeping his paper from him. Two more shipments of napkins had arrived, along with five boxes of paper towels, but no paper. And what Miss Peabody had said was on his mind. Could she be right? Were he and the boys soft and flabby? Maybe the Wizzle System should be revised. And Mr. Sturgeon. What did the Headmaster have against expelling Bruno Walton? The boy was obviously a disruptive influence at Macdonald Hall and had more than once earned a one-way ticket home!

Head spinning, he took out a couple of aspirins and headed for the water cooler.

* * *

Saturday afternoon Bruno and Boots were lying in their room in the tiny space that remained. Fifty-four boxes of inkjet paper took up most of the room. They were stacked everywhere except for the boys' beds and desks, and the entranceway to the washroom.

"Look at it rain," said Boots. "I've never seen such a miserable day in my life. It's dark as night out there."

"Pretty miserable," agreed Bruno. "Foggy, misty, wet —

a real downpour. Too bad Wizzle doesn't have a picnic planned."

"I hope Wizzle doesn't have an inspection planned," said Boots." There's no way all The Committee's task forces combined could get this paper out in time."

"Don't worry about it," said Bruno. "Security knows what they're doing."

"Yeah, well, I'd hate to have my life depend on Wilbur Hackenschleimer, especially if it's suppertime."

"Hey," said Bruno, peering through the streaming window, "something's going on at Scrimmage's."

Boots got up and joined him at the window. "In this miserable downpour? Miss Scrimmage never lets them outside without a written guarantee from the weather bureau."

"All the same, there are people out there around the orchard. I can't see what they're doing. It's too foggy. But it's a big crowd."

"They can't be up to much in this rain," said Boots.

* * *

"What a beautiful day for war games!" exclaimed Miss Peabody in jubilation.

"Beautiful?" echoed Miss Scrimmage. "It's horrible! These are delicate young ladies! They'll catch cold!"

"It's only water, Miss Scrimmage, and a good soaking never hurt anybody. With the fog and the rain, it'll make camouflaging all the easier." She sighed. "If only I could take part."

Miss Peabody addressed the assembled armies. "All right, girls, you'll have fifteen minutes to take up your positions and set up fortifications. Remember, if you're hit with the food colouring, you're a casualty and that's it for you. I'm the referee and I'll be making sure there isn't any funny stuff. All right, you've got fifteen minutes. May the best army win!"

Both armies scattered, the Blue-White toward the northern stronghold, the Red-Green to the south. Miss Peabody listened contentedly to the sound of preparations. She checked her watch. It was one o'clock. The fifteen minutes were up.

"Ten seconds!" she bellowed. Everyone tensed. "*Go!*"

Behind the lines, Cathy and her officers were manning the catapult they had been up all night building. They loaded it with a gigantic plastic bag full of the blue-dyed water and let fly.

There were screams of shock in the ranks of the Red-Green army as the bomb landed among them and splattered blue in all directions.

"*Charge!*" screamed Cathy.

The Blue-White army thundered through the gloom of the orchard, some running, some being pushed in wheelbarrows. The enraged Red-Green army opened fire. Streams of red dye cut into the ranks of the Blue-Whites.

"Hit the dirt!" cried Cathy. The Blue-Whites fell to the soggy ground and began establishing their position along a line in the orchard. The wheelbarrows kept on rolling, driving right into the ranks of the Red-Green army. In the lead barrow General Cathy Burton, a water pistol in each hand, sprayed dye on anything that moved. She paused only occasionally to reach for a dye grenade to throw at enemy pockets.

"*Look out.*"

On the limb of a tree sat a Red-Green sniper. As Cathy's

wheelbarrow surged past, the sniper sloshed down a bucket of red dye.

With a terrified scream, Cathy hurled herself from the barrow to the ground and looked up to see Diane dripping with red dye. Savagely she aimed both her pistols up the tree and shot the sniper down. A stream of red whizzed by her shoulder, missing her, but not by much. She jumped behind the wheelbarrow for cover and began to shoot back.

"I'm running out of ammo!" cried Cathy to Diane. "Give me your gun!"

"I can't! I'm a casualty!"

"Give me your gun!" Cathy ran out from behind the tipped barrow, dodging a barrage of enemy fire, grabbed Diane's pistol and began to shoot her way back to the ranks of her Blue-Whites. Reaching no-man's-land, she made a mad dash and leapt behind a mountain of mud the Blue-White army had built up for cover.

"How's it going?" she asked Ruth Sidwell.

"I've never been so terrified in my life! Where's Diane?"

"Casualty," said Cathy. "But how's it going? Are we winning the war?"

"Who can tell in this mud?"

"We can't use the wheelbarrows anymore!" gasped Wilma Dorf. "They're all bogged down in the mud!" Suddenly a large red bomb exploded in their midst. Ruth and Wilma were hit, but Cathy threw herself aside just in time.

"Retreat!" she howled, pausing to shoot a sniper in a tree. "Regroup at Checkpoint B!"

At Checkpoint B the Blue-White army was hit by a

major enemy offensive. Through a gap in the trees came an onrush of Red-Green troops armed with water pistols and small bombs, carrying large pieces of cardboard for protection.

A small group of defenders retreated, drawing the enemy surge through the thin passageway.

"Attack!" cried Cathy Burton.

From the trees swarms of Blue-Whites appeared, dropping large bombs on the trapped Red-Green forces below. The bewildered Red-Greens fought back as best they could, but were wiped out by superior fire power.

Cathy grabbed the catapult in her arms and the Blue-Whites ran forward to encounter the bulk of the Red-Green army. Onward they charged, slipping and sliding in the mud, wet and filthy, to find that the Red-Greens were gone.

"Oh, those sneaky — " Cathy interrupted herself. "Okay," she whispered. "They're waiting to pounce on us. Now what are we going to do?"

"Occupy all their territory and try to corner them?" asked Janice Adams.

"Nah!" scoffed Cathy. "That's what they're expecting us to do. We're going to sit right here and fortify ourselves. We'll be so strong by the time they come at us that we'll wipe them out."

"I don't understand it," said one of the lieutenants of the Red-Green army. "Why did we leave our position? We could have had them all."

"We were losing too many troops," said the Captain. "Now Burton knows she has three-quarters of the field. She's going to try to corner us. But when she does, she'll spread her forces too thin. We'll just sit here and fortify ourselves, waiting for them to come. And when they do, we'll punch a hole right through their lines and double back and wipe them out!"

* * *

It was four o'clock and the rain was still pouring down. It had been more than two hours since the armies had started the waiting game, and the tension on both sides had reached the breaking point.

Walter C. Wizzle walked across Miss Scrimmage's front lawn carrying his umbrella, intent on visiting Miss Peabody. He had resolved to tell her that she was right about physical fitness, and that he was going to begin morning calisthenics at Macdonald Hall first thing Monday. He was also going to ask her advice on organizing the exercises.

Approaching the school, he was startled to find Miss Scrimmage standing on the front porch dressed in her rain slicker and staring about, wild-eyed.

"Good afternoon, Miss Scrimmage. Is Miss Peabody in?"

"Oh, she's in the orchard!" shrilled the Headmistress. "Oh, how terrible!" She shivered.

"Uh — is something wrong, Miss Scrimmage?" She pointed wordlessly to the apple orchard, face contorted with horror.

Mr. Wizzle made his way to the orchard, a trifle bewildered. What was wrong with Miss Scrimmage? And why would anyone be outside in an apple orchard on a miserable day like today?

He surveyed the orchard. It would be hard to find a person in there. The trees were thick, and it was dark and gloomy. Well, he would just have to walk around. Surely he would run into her eventually.

Cathy sat beside the loaded catapult, an intense expression on her face. Suddenly her eyebrows shot up. "Someone's coming!" she whispered to her troops. "The Red-Green army! Battle stations, everybody! Don't move till I give the word!"

Cathy sat ready, hands shaking with anticipation, until a dim figure appeared through the trees.

"Fire!"

She fired the catapult.

With an enormous splash, the blue-paint bomb shot up and struck Mr. Wizzle full in the face, spinning him around, dazed.

"Attack!" Out of nowhere sloshed a bucket of red dye, registering another direct hit on Mr. Wizzle.

The two armies spied each other and pandemonium broke loose. They surged together, meeting in the middle, knocking Mr. Wizzle over. Red and blue dye was everywhere. Streams from water pistols cut the air like laser beams, bombs large and small were splattering all over, and buckets of dye were splashed in all directions. Both armies plowed back and forth through the mud, stepping over the collapsed figure of Mr. Wizzle.

Casualties piled up quickly as the crazed battle progressed, and the very ground and trees began to look solid red and blue. The melee raged on until it became a shoot-out between Cathy, with one of her lieutenants, and five Red-Green soldiers.

Over her shoulder Cathy saw a stream of red dye strike her companion's back. She was alone. Screaming in defiance, she went up a tree like a monkey and began picking off the enemy, one by one. She caught the last Red-Green with a perfect shot to the centre of the forehead.

Miss Peabody ran onto the scene. "All right! All right! The war's over! Blue-White wins!"

A crazed expression came over Cathy's face as she looked down at the Assistant Headmistress. She would never get another opportunity like this.

"The enemy!" she cried, and squirted Miss Peabody full in the face.

She was out of the tree and disarmed in three seconds.

"All right, everybody!" cried Miss Peabody. "Good workout, all of you! Hit the showers! Burton, I'll see you in my office!" She looked at the ground. One figure did not stir. It was a man covered in dye, mud and grass, holding a mashed umbrella. She grabbed him by the collar and hauled him to his feet.

Mr. Wizzle's eyes uncrossed and he stared into Miss Peabody's blue-dyed face. "Miss Peabody?" he asked feebly.

She laughed. "Boy, Wizzle, did they ever give it to you!"

He was too stunned to argue. "Uh-huh."

"Well, you'd better come in for a while and recover. If we sent you home, you'd never find the place."

Mr. Wizzle was still in a daze. "Was that the big earthquake? Am I dead?"

"No," she laughed, "you're dyed."

"Boy, Burton, you sure know how to gum up a good thing once you've earned it."

Cathy looked at Miss Peabody questioningly.

"That was pretty nice shooting you did there. You

should be proud. You caught Sophie Lipton right between the eyes." She frowned. "You caught Gloria Peabody right between the eyes, too. That was stupid."

Cathy assumed what she hoped was a perfectly innocent expression. "Miss Peabody, I'm terribly sorry about squirting you. You see, I was so caught up in the thrill of battle — "

"Balloonjuice! You saw a way to get even for all those laps I've handed you, and you took it! You only made one mistake. When you shot me, you were shooting the referee. That's something to remember, Burton. Never shoot the referee until the prize is already handed out. No trip."

Cathy was horrified. "No trip? But the girls will kill me!"

Miss Peabody grinned. "I wouldn't worry about that. They'll have to catch you first. And you'll be moving pretty fast — on the track."

Cathy glared her resentment. Well, all right, so there was no prize. But to have given Peabody a faceful of blue dye — it was worth it!

Chapter 11

a star is born

The Committee held a meeting of all major department heads over dinner on Sunday. The dining hall was buzzing with the news that all students were to turn out on the soccer field at 6:30 the next morning for calisthenics.

"I don't see how The Fish could have given Wizzle permission to do this to us!" exclaimed Pete Anderson.

"I don't believe in morning calisthenics," put in Elmer.

"And it leaves so little time for breakfast," mourned Wilbur.

"The last time I tried to do jumping jacks I sprained both ankles," announced Sidney. "I was in a wheelchair for weeks."

Everybody laughed.

"The worst part," put in Larry, "is this: I overheard at the office that Miss Peabody is coming over from Scrimmage's to help out!"

"Oh, no!" moaned Sidney.

"Wait a minute!" said Bruno. "I've got an idea. This could be a really big thing for us. Tomorrow morning we'll all go out and do Wizzle's calisthenics."

"What's so good about that?" asked Boots. "Do we have a choice?"

"We do the calisthenics," explained Bruno, "and then we ask to do more. Then we all request that we repeat our *personal* favourite exercises. We just keep asking to do more and more exercises . . . "

* * *

Morning calisthenics began at 6:30 with Mr. Wizzle and Miss Peabody standing up at the front of the Macdonald Hall student body. They began with jumping jacks, jogging in place, push-ups and sit-ups. At 6:40, Mr. Wizzle announced, "That's enough for today. You can go."

Bruno's hand shot up. "Mr. Wizzle, sir, let's do that again."

"All of it?" asked Mr. Wizzle incredulously.

"Yes, sir," said Bruno enthusiastically. There were cheers from the assembled students.

Mr. Wizzle and Miss Peabody led them through the ten-minute routine again.

Boots's hand shot up. "Mr. Wizzle, sir, let's have a morning run."

"Well," said Mr. Wizzle, breathing heavily, "we don't want to overdo it the first day and —"

"Come on, Wizzle," said Miss Peabody, "if they're enthusiastic, so much the better."

"Okay," he said. "Where do you want to run?"

"Around the campus," called Pete Anderson. The other boys cheered their approval.

Mr. Wizzle was horrified. "But it's a big campus and — uh — " He withered under Miss Peabody's gaze. "Okay, let's run around the campus."

"Three times!" called Chris Talbot. More approving cheers came from the boys.

With Mr. Wizzle and Miss Peabody in the lead, the boys began running around the perimeter of the campus. By the time they had finished three circuits, it was seven-twenty.

Mr. Wizzle was hyperventilating. "Okay, now I guess we can all go and —"

"Mr. Wizzle," piped Larry Wilson, "we didn't do enough jumping jacks. That's my favourite."

A number of boys called out in agreement.

"Well, we really have been at this a while and —"

"If they want to do them, Wizzle — " began Miss Peabody sternly.

"Okay," puffed Mr. Wizzle. "More jumping jacks."

They did jumping jacks until 7:30.

"Okay," called Mr. Wizzle, gasping for breath, "we've done a lot so — uh" — he looked at them hopefully — "if there are no more requests — "

"Sit-ups!" called Bruno.

"Push-ups!" added Boots.

"Knee bends!" piped Wilbur.

"Toe touches!"

"Side-bends!"

"Leg lifts!"

At quarter to eight the group was still doing push-ups. At eight o'clock they were doing stretching exercises. At 8:15 they were on their backs bicycling, and at 8:20 Mr. Wizzle collapsed in a heap.

"I can't do any more!" he croaked at Miss Peabody, his voice a rasp.

"Dismissed!" she bellowed. "Come on now, Wizzle. Get up."

"I can't!"

"All right," she said, hauling him to his feet. "Let's go. Say, I was pretty impressed with those boys. They must be in better shape than I thought. One thing's sure — they're in better shape than you are."

He was too weak to reply.

Bruno and Boots staggered into their room and fell onto their beds.

"Heart attack!" breathed Bruno. "My aching bones!"

"I'm definitely dying!" gasped Boots.

"Well, at least we have the consolation of knowing that Wizzle is, too."

"Leg cramp!" howled Boots.

"Me, too!" said Bruno in a strained voice. "But I'll bet Wizzle's are worse."

Boots snorted. "And it didn't help matters much to stay up all night shaking Wizzle's house. While we were seeing to it that he got no sleep, we didn't get any either. And we've got to go to class in half an hour."

"Oh," moaned Bruno. "But at least Wizzle won't be sitting in on any classes today."

Cathy and Diane sat huddled in blankets in their room, their feet in a large basin of hot water. After the war games, the entire student body of Miss Scrimmage's Finishing School for Young Ladies had come down with colds.

Diane sneezed violently and reached for a tissue. "I still don't understand how you could have blown our trip! If the girls ever get well, they're going to kill you!"

Cathy's face assumed a dreamy, far-off look. "But it was so wonderful. How could anyone in my place resist it? She was there, and I gave it to her right in the kisser. It was the most beautiful two seconds of my life."

"Yeah, well, for those two seconds you blew two beautiful days away from Peabody for a hundred and fifty people. How many laps did she give you?"

"Ten," said Cathy, "But I'll never have to do them." She coughed. "I'll fake sick for a while."

"Like for eight months?" asked Diane.

"Peabody's going to be gone before that," said Cathy confidently. "I haven't stopped trying to get rid of her. I just got sidetracked. She definitely goes before we have to suffer through her next brilliant plan."

"Well, you'd better hurry," sniffled Diane. "I overheard that we're going on some kind of a march next weekend."

"Oh, no way! There's no way I'm doing anything else military! I'm a civilian!"

Diane sighed. "Tell that to Peabody."

* * *

"The jig's up," said Larry Wilson the next day at lunch. "Wizzle's got inkjet paper. He's in there now printing out reports like it's going out of style."

"How'd that happen?" asked Bruno, annoyed.

"This morning he drove down to Systems Supply Ltd. and fought with them so much that they let him into the warehouse to stuff three boxes personally."

"Well, we'll just have to replace them, won't we?" decided Bruno. "We can give him more paper towels."

"It's not that easy," said Larry. "When he went home for lunch he carried all the paper with him. He's not letting it out of his sight."

"Are you sure we couldn't maybe nab it when he's not looking?" asked Bruno hopefully.

"No way. He watched it like a hawk all morning." Larry laughed. "Looked kind of weird."

"All right," said Bruno, "Operation Shut-Up is over. It sure was great while it lasted."

"It isn't over in our room," put in Boots. "What are we going to do with all that paper?"

"Wizzle wants it," said Bruno. "We'll give it back to him. The Security Department will help us move it into the Faculty Building tonight. Right, Wilbur?"

"Okay," conceded Wilbur between bites.

"Now," said Bruno, "what are we going to do to replace Operation Shut-Up now that Wizzle's back in business?"

"How about we take a break?" called Mark Davies. "It won't get rid of Wizzle, but it'll give the Lines Department a chance to catch up. Besides, I'm still stiff from yesterday morning's calisthenics. The next time you decide to exercise Wizzle into the ground, Bruno, count me out."

There were catcalls of agreement which spread to many of the other tables.

"I believe that those exercises were instrumental in the dislocation of my sacroiliac joint," put in Elmer.

"Never mind that," said Bruno. "How's the balloon coming along?"

"The inflater is finished," said Elmer, "and I happen to have a spare compressed-helium tank left over from my lighter-than-air experiments."

"But it's taking a lot of time to put together all that vinyl," added Chris. "The Balloon Department's been working in the gym every night, but it's a big job."

"Don't worry about the time," said Bruno. "Just keep up the good work. We need an idea for now."

"*I* need an idea for now," said Pete mournfully. "I'm editor of the school newspaper, remember? Wizzle expects to see the paper tomorrow and I haven't started it yet. I don't even have any articles. Nobody ever does anything worth writing about around here."

"When I was editor, I never missed an issue," said Mark sourly.

"Hey, don't rub it in," moaned Pete. "I just wish someone would do something really — uh — something — "

"Newsworthy," said Mark.

"Yeah."

Bruno had a thoughtful expression on his face which changed to a grin that matched the dancing of his eyes. "I know someone who did something newsworthy. G. Gavin Gunhold."

"Yeah!" exclaimed Pete enthusiastically, whipping out a notebook and pencil and writing the name down. His brows furrowed. "Uh — who's G. Gavin Gunhold?"

"Isn't that the phony name you signed on the delivery

ticket for some of Wizzle's paper?" asked Boots.

"G. Gavin Gunhold," announced Bruno, "is Macdonald Hall's foremost student. He is a model young man. He is a star athlete, a scholar, a student leader, a youth action politician and everything else noble and good. And Wizzle's never heard of him."

"Bruno, what are you talking about?" asked Boots irritably. "Why are you making up this creep?"

"When Wizzle finds out that he doesn't know our best student," explained Bruno, "he'll move heaven and earth to find the guy. And when he can't, it'll drive him nuts."

"It won't work, Bruno," said Larry. "The Fish or one of the teachers is bound to tell him there is no G. Gavin Gunhold."

"He won't even ask," replied Bruno, "because his own brainchild, WizzleWare, is going to have a full record of G. Gavin Gunhold. Elmer, can you do it?"

"What? You mean program this person into the student records?"

"Yeah," said Bruno. "Tonight when we deliver the paper. Elmer'll come with us and program Gunhold into the computer. A star is born!"

"What about my newspaper?" asked Pete in distress.

"Boots and I aren't busy," Bruno replied. "We'll help you. We can write some articles on the achievements of G. Gavin Gunhold." He pounded the table. "All right, you guys. Operation Gunhold is now on."

* * *

Carrying a box of his precious inkjet paper, Mr. Wizzle bounced energetically into the school's outer office and stopped short. His jaw dropped and the carton in his

134

hands fell to the floor with a thump. There, piled in and around his desk, almost completely hiding it from view, were dozens of boxes of paper.

"Where the devil — "

"Planning to work overtime, Wizzle?"

Mr. Wizzle wheeled to see the Headmaster standing behind him. "Uh — Mr. Sturgeon — did you see any of this arrive?"

"It was here this morning when I came in," said Mr. Sturgeon. "Mrs. Davis counted fifty-four boxes. A bit expensive, don't you think?"

"Well — uh — you see, they kept sending me toilet paper and napkins, and I guess yesterday they realized — and they sent — I'll have some of it sent back."

"Good idea," said Mr. Sturgeon, walking into his office.

Resolving to give Systems Supply Ltd. a piece of his mind, Mr. Wizzle set about clearing a path through the cartons to his office. He entered and saw a copy of the school newspaper sitting on his desk. So Anderson had come through, he thought with satisfaction. He had been dead right about Anderson then. Give a boy enough responsibility and he will rise to meet the challenge.

He sat down and looked at the headline:

GUNHOLD WINS CHAMPIONSHIP

He frowned. What could this be about?

> Macdonald Hall superstar G. Gavin Gunhold showed excellent form in winning the Ontario Junior Track and Field Championship in Hamilton last week. Out of the nine events, Gunhold won five, placed second in three

more, and third in the last, to capture the trophy.

"I'm really pleased," said Gunhold in an interview . . .

Mr. Wizzle skipped to another article down the page.

PARK CLEAN-UP PROGRAM A SUCCESS

York County Parks and Recreation Department expressed
their gratitude to G. Gavin Gunhold and the group of
Macdonald Hall students who ran the anti-litter campaign
at Bruce's Mill Park . . .

Mr. Wizzle opened to page two.

YORK ACADEMY CHESSMASTER DEFEATED

Macdonald Hall chess champion G. Gavin Gunhold
brought the Hartley Trophy back to Macdonald Hall in
triumph last week, soundly defeating York Academy's
Stanley Wump four games straight in a best-of-seven
series. "It's about time," Gunhold was quoted as saying . . .

And on page three:

MACDONALD HALL BAND PLACES SECOND

The Macdonald Hall marching band took second place
honors in the region last week, coming in close behind
Humberland Collegiate. Macdonald Hall did pick up one
first, though, as the soloist prize was decisively won by
G. Gavin Gunhold on the oboe. "We should have won the
whole thing," Gunhold said afterwards, "but I'm still
pleased . . .

Mr. Wizzle frowned. How was it that he had never noticed this boy Gunhold? He left his office, cleared away some of the boxes, and sat down at the computer. He typed Gunhold's name and clicked SEARCH.

```
Gunhold, G. Gavin
Status: Senior
Height: 1.88 m
Weight: 77 kg
Eyes: Blue
Hair: Blond
Dental record: Perfect
Allergies: None
Academic average: 94.7%
Percentile: 99
Demerits: 0
Psychological profile: Stable; excellent
adjustment
Career recommendation: Medicine
Special achievements:
```

A long list of G. Gavin Gunhold's honours and awards followed.

Mr. Wizzle sat back thoughtfully. How was it that he'd never heard of this boy? A giddy memory came to him suddenly, the memory of a heated conversation with Systems Supply Ltd. They'd said that G. Gavin Gunhold had signed for the first shipment of paper. The boy certainly seemed to get around.

Chapter 12

g. gavin gunhold is dead

"William, who is G. Gavin Gunhold?"

Mr. Sturgeon smiled at his wife. "Oh, you read the paper, did you? I think G. Gavin Gunhold is a joke, Mildred. Wizzle made Anderson editor of the school paper and Anderson doesn't know what to put in a newspaper, so I suppose a group of the boys got together and thought up G. Gavin Gunhold. It's quite clever, actually."

"It isn't right," she said primly. "It's expensive to put out a newspaper, and it shouldn't be wasted on nonsense."

"You haven't seen wasted paper until you've seen Wizzle. He had fifty-four cartons of the stuff piled in the office this morning. Anyway, there's no harm in G. Gavin Gunhold. The boys have to report something."

138

She sighed. "In a way it's a shame it isn't all true. He certainly sounds like a wonderful boy."

* * *

Bruno and Boots were walking with Pete Anderson down the hall of the Faculty Building when Mr. Wizzle approached them.

"Ah, Anderson, I've been looking all over for you. An excellent job you did on the paper. I especially liked the articles on Gavin Gunhold."

"Thank you, sir," stammered Pete.

"By the way, boys, have any of you seen Gunhold today?" Boots and Pete both turned pale.

"Uh — Gavin just walked out of biology class," supplied Bruno. "He was headed for the English wing, I think."

"Thanks." Mr. Wizzle trotted off.

Boots and Pete exhaled simultaneously.

* * *

Mr. Wizzle sat at his desk. How distressing! He had wasted a whole day looking for G. Gavin Gunhold with no success — the boy was nowhere to be found. It seemed that everywhere Mr. Wizzle inquired, he had just missed him by five minutes. He had even checked with Elmer Drimsdale, Gunhold's roommate, but Drimsdale had said that Gavin was always busy, always on the move. There was something strange about that. From past dormitory inspections Mr. Wizzle could have sworn Drimsdale lived alone. Yet there were two beds, two desks, two dressers and two sets of clothing in the closet. Gunhold lived in 201 all right.

He noticed a letter on the corner of his desk and reached for it. The letterhead (printed not an hour earlier in the Macdonald Hall print shop) read:

The Caldwell Foundation, Edmonton, Alberta

Dear Sir,

It is my distinct pleasure to inform you
that one of your students, G. Gavin Gunhold,
has won this year's Caldwell Foundation Medal
for his paper on patriotism. A ticket will be
waiting for Mr. Gunhold at Magellan Airlines
Booth 11, Toronto International Airport, and
we expect to see him at our awards dinner.

Mr. Wizzle stared at the date. Heavens! It was on Saturday! If he didn't find Gunhold immediately, the boy might miss being present to accept his award!

Quickly he dashed off a note and called for the messenger.

"Yes, sir?" said Larry Wilson.

"Take this over to room 201 and see that Gavin Gunhold gets it. It's of the utmost importance." Larry ran down the hall and out the door of the Faculty Building only to collapse in fits of helpless laughter on the front lawn.

* * *

By Thursday night Mr. Wizzle was no less than frantic. He had been checking around all day and Gunhold was nowhere to be found. All the boys he'd asked claimed that Gunhold was on a special field trip but would be home for dinner. Wizzle had gone to the dining hall at six o'clock only to be told that Gunhold was working in the chemistry lab, which was closed. Finally one boy had mentioned that Gunhold had organized a small group of boys who had been given special permission to go off-campus to one of the local farms to help out an ailing farmer. They would be back by lights-out. Wizzle had left a strict message with Drimsdale that Gunhold was to call him immediately at home.

At two minutes to ten the telephone rang in Mr. Wizzle's cottage. He ran for the phone, but as he took his first step a strong earth tremor hit the house. He stopped indecisively, torn between his duty to a student and his own personal safety. The phone rang again and he took a step toward it. Suddenly the tremor became stronger and he thought he saw a new crack appearing in the plaster. His mind made up, Mr. Wizzle sprinted to the door and rushed outside. He paused to catch his breath. Inside, the ringing stopped.

He rushed across the campus toward Dormitory 2, wondering idly why Wilbur Hacken was always standing out in the open blowing his nose. He rushed inside and began pounding on the door of room 201.

Elmer answered the door. "Oh, Mr. Wizzle. Did Gavin get in touch with you?"

"No, he didn't! Where is he?"

"The boys he was with came back," explained Elmer, "but Gavin is going to stay the night. He's got special permission to miss his morning classes tomorrow." He frowned. "He said he was going to call you. I guess you must have been out."

"Uh — yes. Yes, I was out. Well, go to bed, Drimsdale. I'll catch Gunhold later."

Mr. Wizzle ran out of the dormitory and back across the lawn. This whole G. Gavin Gunhold thing was beginning to get to him. Why, if he hadn't seen the complete records on the boy, he'd swear that Gunhold didn't even exist! Coming on top of those earthquakes, that miserable foul-up with the printer paper, his horrible accident at Scrimmage's and those terrible calisthenics, this was just too much.

He ran up to Mr. Sturgeon's front porch and rang the bell insistently.

The Headmaster opened the door. "Hello, Wizzle. Come in. What can I do for you?"

Mr. Wizzle walked in, his face wild. "Mr. Sturgeon, I've spent all week looking for G. Gavin Gunhold and I can't find him anywhere!"

"Well, that's understandable," said Mr. Sturgeon.

Mr. Wizzle looked at him. "Yes — uh — every time I look for him he's either just left or is off-campus by special permission! He's never at class, although his record says he's a straight-A student! And now he's won the Caldwell Foundation Medal for his paper on patriotism, and his plane for Edmonton is leaving tomorrow afternoon, but he doesn't know about it because he's at some farmer's house helping out! Mr. Sturgeon, what am I going to do?"

Mr. Sturgeon led him into the neat kitchen. "Sit down, Wizzle," he said kindly.

The two men sat down at the table.

"Wizzle, there is no such person as G. Gavin Gunhold."

Mr. Wizzle went white. "But — but there has to be! The computer has a file on him!"

"Then someone else fed it in. I can assure you there is no G. Gavin Gunhold. He has no academic record; he didn't win a track meet, a chess tournament, or a foundation medal; he doesn't play the oboe and he isn't out assisting farmers. He just *isn't*, Wizzle. It's as simple as that."

Mr. Wizzle looked sick. All he could manage to say was, "I don't understand."

"I'm afraid the entire thing is a hoax," explained Mr. Sturgeon.

Mr. Wizzle leapt to his feet, his face flaming. "The nerve! Just wait till I get my hands on the boys responsible! Drimsdale! I'll expel Drimsdale! And Anderson! And Walton! I told you about Walton! He said Gunhold was a close friend of his! Yes, and Wilson — !"

"Calm down for a moment, Wizzle," said the Headmaster, "and answer a question for me, please. In all your inquiries, did even one boy deny knowing Gunhold?"

"Well — uh — no."

"Then obviously all the boys were in on the joke. And you cannot expel everyone or hand out thousands of demerits. Wizzle, the two of us might not agree on some matters of education, but there is one thing of which I can assure you after years of experience as an educator: No matter how strictly or how well you enforce discipline, there are always going to be practical jokes. And this one, if you will forgive my saying so, has been rather magnificent."

"You're on their side!" stormed Mr. Wizzle.

"Most assuredly I am. They're my boys. A word of advice: If you rant and rave and make a big fuss about this it will all be part of the joke and they'll laugh even harder. But if you take it like a man and come up smiling, they'll respect you for it. Let me handle this."

Mr. Wizzle inhaled deeply. "I suppose you might have a point there." His voice rose again. "But I really don't think I have to tolerate — "

"Wizzle," said the Headmaster patiently.

"Well, how about — "

"No."

"Oh, all right!"

Mrs. Sturgeon appeared in the doorway. "William, what's — Oh, hello, Mr. Wizzle. Would you like some tea?"

"Yes, please," he answered faintly.

Mr. Sturgeon was disposed to be kind. "Don't take it so hard, Wizzle. They once switched my tuxedo for a judo suit on Founders' Day."

* * *

Bruno had gone to sleep laughing and he woke up laughing.

"I just can't wait to see what G. Gavin Gunhold is going to do next," he chuckled to Boots. "You know, when he gets back from helping the farmer."

Boots began to dress. "Maybe we should downplay G. Gavin Gunhold a little. We're in for a lot of trouble if we get caught."

"Are you nuts? It's going perfectly. Will he make it to Edmonton in time to receive his award? Maybe we should send him to Europe or something, or to New York to mediate in United Nations debates. How about we make him special emissary to the Vatican?"

"Calm down, Bruno," grinned Boots.

"It almost makes me sad that Wizzle will have to leave," said Bruno. "I've never had so much fun in my life. It reminds me of the good old days."

There was a knock on the door. Boots opened it to admit Larry Wilson. Larry looked worried.

"Hey, you guys, The Fish wants to see both of you right away."

"Oh, no!" gasped Boots.

"We're on our way," said Bruno. "I wonder what he wants? What have we done lately?"

"What *haven't* we done lately?" snapped Boots. "Do you think he's found out about The Committee?"

"No. How could he? The Security Department would never allow that. Anyway, don't worry. Whatever it is, we'll bluff our way through it."

Boots shook his head. "This isn't Wizzle, Bruno! It's The Fish! He's going to kill us if he's found out about The Committee!"

"Come on," said Bruno stepping into his shoes.

"Let's find out what this is all about."

Boots just moaned.

The two boys ran across the campus to the Faculty Building, rushed inside and tapped on Mr. Sturgeon's door.

"Have a seat." Mr. Sturgeon motioned toward the decidedly uncomfortable wooden bench reserved for students called on the carpet.

"Walton, O'Neal," he began grimly, "I have some distressing news for you. G. Gavin Gunhold is dead." He paused for effect, noting with satisfaction their stricken expressions.

Bruno studied the carpet, then looked up. "Uh — how did you know it was us, sir?"

"When has it ever been anyone else?" retorted Mr. Sturgeon. "Although this time I must admit that you have dragged an inordinate number of people into your unworthy scheming. Do you realize that Drimsdale and Anderson could be in serious trouble because of this?"

Both boys gazed at the floor.

"This hoax is responsible for wasting" — he paused to choose his words carefully — "a good deal of staff time. It may seem like a great joke to you. There are some of us, however, who are not amused."

He began pacing up and down in front of them. "In addition, I am certain that, were I to investigate Mr. Wizzle's recent problem with paper delivery, I would find you at the bottom of it. You can thank your lucky stars that I have no proof of this." He fell silent, debating whether or not to mention Mr. Wizzle's earthquake problem. He decided against it. After all, it was obviously impossible for schoolboys — even seven hundred of them — to create earthquakes. Besides, how could Wizzle be having earthquakes which were not affecting the whole area? Better not to mention the earthquakes.

"Are you going to give us demerits, sir?" asked Bruno, thinking securely of the Lines Department.

"No," said the Headmaster shortly. "You will each deliver to me in one week's time a one-thousand-word essay on the morality of practical jokes. I am assigning Drimsdale and Anderson the same."

Bruno's mind raced. Could The Committee set up an Essay Department?

"You are dismissed," said Mr. Sturgeon. "Please bear in mind that if you are called into my office on this subject again, things will go very hard with you. Good day."

Bruno and Boots fled.

"Just like the good old days!" mimicked Boots savagely. "Just like the *bad* good old days!"

* * *

Cathy Burton lay on her bed feeling as stiff as a board. As soon as she had recovered from her post-war-games cold, Miss Peabody had pounced on her to do the ten punishment laps.

"The march starts at seven o'clock tomorrow morning," Diane was saying, "and she says it's going to be around forty kilometres."

Cathy sat up with an audible creak. "Forty kilometres? Is she nuts?"

"Forty kilometres. That's what Peabody said," confirmed Diane. "Over rough terrain. She said we'd get back sometime in the early evening."

"Well, I don't care what Peabody said," announced Cathy. "There is no power in the universe that can make me go on a forced march!"

* * *

"Okay, fall in for the march!" bellowed Miss Peabody.

The scorching sun of Indian summer beat heavily down on the girls of Miss Scrimmage's. It was the hottest day of the fall.

"Thought you weren't coming," commented Diane as Cathy hefted her backpack.

"Leave me alone," growled Cathy. "I'm dying."

"All right — forward, *march!* Hut, two, three, four! Hut, two, three, four! Come on, look alive, Burton!"

"If I survive this," muttered Cathy darkly, "which I doubt, Peabody will rue this march. Maybe a nice long walk will give me a chance to plan some strategy."

"The last time you planned strategy," said Diane, we all ran a lot of laps."

"Shhh," said Cathy. "I'm detaching my mind from my body."

* * *

A practical joke is funny, but sometimes it's not so funny, wrote Pete Anderson. "Hmmm. Eleven words."

Pete, Elmer, Bruno and Boots were sprawled in various poses around room 306 writing their punishment essays.

"I still say we should have formed a department or sub-committee or something to do this," said Bruno. "I mean, we shouldn't be wasting our time. We're important officials of The Committee."

"We're going to do the essays ourselves and stay out of trouble," said Boots. "You can fool Wizzle, but you can't fool The Fish."

"And we did deserve it," added Elmer. "Mr. Sturgeon is always very fair."

"Fair to poor," admitted Bruno grudgingly.

"Huh!" snorted Pete. "If there's one thing I hate more than doing tests, it's writing essays. Hey, Boots, how many words have you got? I've got eleven."

"I haven't counted."

"How about this?" said Pete. *"A practical joke isn't funny unless everyone's laughing. For example, when Mr. Wizzle isn't laughing, nobody's laughing."*

"I suggest that you revise that," said Elmer seriously. "What Mr. Sturgeon wants is a general critique on the morality of practical jokes, not specific examples."

"Oh, yeah," said Pete, drawing a line through his last two sentences. "That leaves me with — let's see — eleven words."

"Ah," said Elmer with an elaborate pen stroke. "Finished."

"Me, too," said Boots. "I don't think I'm up to a thousand words, but it's close enough."

"Oh," said Pete brightly. "You mean you don't really have to have a thousand words?" His face fell. "Yeah, but I'm pretty sure you need more than eleven."

"Probably," grinned Boots.

"Come on, Pete," said Bruno, "just write any old thing down."

* * *

It was half past eight when the forced march finally ended at the front gate of Miss Scrimmage's Finishing School for Young Ladies.

"Okay, girls," sang out Miss Peabody, her step still springy, "well done. Because of today's good effort, there will be no calisthenics tomorrow. You can sleep until nine."

There were a few weak, hoarse cheers.

"I'll get her for this!" rasped Cathy. "My feet are gone! Gone!"

"They're still there," confirmed Diane, looking down.

"I can't feel them!"

"You're lucky," said Diane. "I can feel mine and they hurt. All I want to do is get back to our room and sleep."

"Well, you're not going to sleep," said Cathy. "No one is."

"What?"

"I'll explain it when we get back to our room." The two walked into the residence hall, went up the stairs and entered their room.

"Okay," said Diane, "before I fall asleep I want a full explanation of why I can't."

"Tomorrow morning at the crack of dawn," said Cathy, "in a showing of solidarity against Peabody, we're all going to run away from school."

"Are you crazy?"

"Nope," said Cathy, beginning to undress. "We'll tell all the girls right after I soak in a hot bath." She grabbed a towel and disappeared into the bathroom.

"Wait a minute!" cried Diane. "Where are we going to go?"

She could barely hear Cathy's answer over the sound of running water. "Macdonald Hall."

* * *

It was 5:30 in the morning when Bruno and Boots were awakened by a tapping at their window. The two boys got up and looked out to see Cathy and Diane crouched there.

"Go away!" Boots hissed nervously. "We're in enough trouble!"

"Come on in," invited Bruno. He helped the two girls into the room. "What's up?"

Cathy batted her eyes innocently. "We are two poor waifs who ask only for a place to rest our weary bones."

"What are you babbling about?" asked Boots, slightly hysterical.

"We've run away from school," said Diane.

"What? Both of you?"

"No," said Cathy. "All of us."

"Who else is there?" asked Bruno.

"Everybody," said Cathy. "They're waiting in the woods."

Boots went white. "You mean there are three hundred girls hiding in our woods?"

"Yeah," said Cathy. "We need someplace to hide out until we've decided where to go." She smiled. "And I wouldn't mind something to eat."

"We can't do it!" squeaked Boots. "We have no room for three hundred extra people!"

Cathy's face fell. "Well, we really have nowhere else to go — " she began pitifully.

"Have no fear," said Bruno. "The Committee is here."

"Oh, no, Bruno!" moaned Boots. "Not The Committee! If The Fish — "

"What's The Committee?" asked Diane.

"Only the most sophisticated, well-organized operation in existence," boasted Bruno. "I'll wake up some of the major department heads and we'll form an Emergency Housing Task Force. We'll have all the girls sheltered in no time." He grinned at Cathy. "And we should be able to coax Wilbur Hackenschleimer into raiding the kitchen. He doesn't take much convincing."

"We'll never get away with this, Bruno!" said Boots.

"When a friend asks for help," lectured Bruno, "you can put yourself out a little. Come on. Let's go wake up Wilbur to give the signal."

Chapter 13

the coalition

Mr. Sturgeon had made it his habit to sleep in on Sunday mornings, but that morning he was awakened shortly after nine by a distressing noise. He got up, donned his red silk bathrobe and his bedroom slippers and peered out the window.

An appalling sight met his eyes. There in the open area in front of the dormitories stood Gloria Peabody, ramrod straight, barking orders at the top of her lungs. He stared. Girls seemed to be coming out of his dormitories! Dozens of them! No, hundreds! Miss Scrimmage was also on the scene, running around shrieking and wringing her hands. Wizzle was there too, standing beside Miss Peabody. He seemed to be talking to her, but he was also shouting in the direction of the dormitories.

The Headmaster ran down the stairs and burst out of his front door. He sped across the campus toward the ruckus.

Miss Peabody's voice was deafening. "All right, get out of there! On the double!"

"Oh, girls, girls! Please come out!" shrilled Miss Scrimmage. "Oh, *please!*"

Some more girls came wandering out through the dormitory doors.

"Come on! Hurry it up! Get back to school! *Move!*"

"Boys," called Mr. Wizzle, "you will do nothing to interfere with the evacuation! Assist the girls out of the dormitories!"

"Back to school!" Miss Peabody barked at another group. "You're confined to quarters!"

"Don't forget to eat a good breakfast first!" added Miss Scrimmage.

"Wizzle, what is going on here?" demanded Mr. Sturgeon.

Miss Scrimmage rushed up to the Headmaster. "Your terrible boys kidnapped my poor defenceless girls!"

"Well, we're really sorry, Miss Scrimmage," began Mr. Wizzle, "and — "

"Don't apologize, Wizzle," said Mr. Sturgeon coldly. "Miss Scrimmage's girls are quite capable of taking care of themselves. If they are in our dormitories, rest assured that that is where they choose to be."

"Come on! Move it!" shouted Miss Peabody as more girls trickled out.

In room 306 Boots noted how Diane cringed each time

Miss Peabody's voice rang out. The four had spent the past few hours filling each other in on recent happenings at the two schools.

"You're a great storyteller, Cathy," Bruno approved. "I especially liked the part where you all gave it to Wizzle in the war games."

"And you're an organizational genius, Bruno," said Cathy sincerely. "The Committee is a work of art."

"Hurry it up, girls!" came Miss Peabody's voice.

"Boys," called Mr. Wizzle, "help the girls outside. Miss Peabody is waiting."

"Waiting to pounce," added Diane fearfully.

Cathy sneaked a look out the window at Mr. Wizzle and Miss Peabody, side by side, shouting orders. "Look at those two!" she snorted in disgust. "They're made for each other! They should get married! Why ruin two schools?"

Bruno's eyes bulged. "That's it!"

"That's what?" asked Boots suspiciously.

"That's how we're going to get rid of Wizzle and Peabody! We'll marry them off! Then they'll go off into the sunset and leave us alone!"

Cathy broke into a wide grin. "Bruno, you're a genius!"

"It was your idea," said Bruno generously. "That's right! In that case, *I'm* a genius!"

Outside, Mr. Wizzle turned to Miss Peabody. "I think that's all of them," he said.

"All except Burton and Grant," said Miss Peabody. "Where are they?"

"Follow me," said Mr. Sturgeon wearily. He walked to Dormitory 3 and tapped on a window. "Walton," he said with mock politeness, "would you be so kind as to send

Miss Burton and Miss Grant out immediately?"

Bruno's face appeared at the window. "Yes, sir."

Cathy appeared beside him. "Hi, Mr. Sturgeon. Long time no see." She spied Miss Peabody and ducked down again.

"Burton, get out here! And bring Grant with you!"

"Walton, O'Neal," said Mr. Wizzle sternly, "you've been harbouring them in your room! Ten demerits!"

Cathy and Diane scrambled over the window ledge, and Miss Peabody began running them home.

"That was really stupid, Burton! Really stupid!"

"But Miss Peabody," Cathy protested, "how could you possibly know that I'm responsible?"

"I've got a gut feeling about you, Burton. The whole school's going to run a lot of laps because of this."

Cathy was too happy to worry about laps. She was already planning the wedding.

* * *

Bruno and Boots sat on the bench in Mr. Sturgeon's office.

"I am not going to ask you to explain the presence of Miss Scrimmage's students in our dormitories," began the Headmaster. "I would not force my students to dignify the gross misbehaviour of others with an explanation." He cleared his throat. "I would like to speak to you on a matter that is of much greater importance. Of late, especially in the aftermath of this morning's events, I have been hearing something around this campus which has become almost a catch phrase: The Committee."

Boots turned suddenly white, and even Bruno paled a little.

"Ah," said the Headmaster. "I see the name is familiar to you. You will forgive me for immediately associating you with this committee, but you must admit that in the past such activity has usually found you at the hub. And said activity generally culminates in a good deal of heartache for all concerned."

He leaned back in his chair. "Walton, O'Neal — What *is* The Committee?"

Boots was too stricken to speak.

Bruno cleared his throat. "Well, sir, one day a group of us got together and — uh — formed The Committee."

"I suspected that much. But for what purpose? What is the goal of The Committee?"

"Well," said Bruno carefully, "we all work together to — uh — see to it that Macdonald Hall remains the wonderful place to go to school that it always was."

"I see," said Mr. Sturgeon. "So I suspected. The object of your group is to harass Mr. Wizzle. Am I correct?"

"I guess it sort of looks that way, sir," Bruno admitted.

The Headmaster nodded. "And The Committee was no doubt behind *The Macdonald Hall Free Press?* And the computer paper shortage? And the sudden burst of student energy during calisthenics? And, of course, our man Gunhold?"

Both boys nodded miserably.

Mr. Sturgeon sighed. "Boys, it is a fact of life that things change in the normal course of events. Sometimes we like the changes; sometimes we do not. But we must accept them and learn to live with them. Do you understand?"

Bruno and Boots nodded again.

"Very well. I assume that you two are very high officials

in The Committee. You will go and disband it immediately. There will be no more Committee. Is that clear?"

"Yes, sir."

"Fine. If there are any more complaints of harassment from Mr. Wizzle and you are found responsible, your punishment will be very severe, and your parents will be notified of your activities. Dismissed."

Bruno and Boots left the office and crossed the campus, not daring to speak until they were safely inside room 306.

"I don't understand how The Fish always seems to know exactly what we're doing!" exclaimed Boots, still trembling.

"Yeah," said Bruno. "Hey, we've got to get together with our department heads and talk about how we're going to marry off Wizzle."

"But Bruno," protested Boots, "we promised The Fish we'd disband The Committee!"

"Oh, this isn't The Committee," explained Bruno reasonably. "We're working with Scrimmage's now. It's kind of a coalition. Yeah, that's it. It's The Coalition. You didn't hear The Fish tell us to disband The Coalition, did you?"

"Well, no," said Boots, "but it's the same thing. And we're not allowed to bug Wizzle."

"We're not bugging him," said Bruno righteously. "We're arranging for his lifelong happiness. Someday he'll thank us for it."

"We're not going to get away with this, you know, Bruno."

"Of course we are! We're The Committee — I mean, The Coalition! Right now let's get over to The Coalition Lines

Department. We've got some work for them. And tonight we'll have to consult with Cathy and Diane to figure out our strategy."

* * *

It was just after midnight. Bruno and Boots climbed up the drainpipe, and Cathy and Diane helped them into the room.

"Hi," Cathy greeted them. "Glad you could make it. We're really excited about joining The Committee."

"Sorry," said Boots, "The Committee doesn't exist anymore."

"You've stopped The Committee?" asked Diane in surprise.

"Sort of," said Bruno. "Actually, we've just changed the name. You can't join The Committee, but you've already joined The Coalition."

"We have?" asked Diane.

"Sure," said Bruno. "You have to join. Without you it's not a coalition — it's a committee. Anyway, we came over here to have a conference. How do we get Wizzle and Peabody to the altar?"

"We've been talking about that," said Cathy, "and we've drawn a blank. Wouldn't life be simpler if we could just give them a love potion?"

"Forget it," laughed Boots. "Even Elmer Drimsdale couldn't concoct a potion like that!"

"What a drag," said Cathy. "Well, then, we'll just have to convince Peabody that there is no one more handsome, more debonair, more devastating, or more sexy than Wizzle."

"Right," grinned Bruno. "And we'll convince Wizzle that

there's no one more beautiful, more graceful, more charming, or more desirable than Peabody." He made a face. "How are we going to do that?"

"Little gifts, big hints," said Cathy. "Just remember to be subtle. I'm sure you two Romeos will be able to figure it out. After all, you're The Committee."

"The Coalition," Bruno corrected.

"Yeah, well anyway, Peabody was out this afternoon and that gave us a chance to raid the kitchen, so we've got some food. Care for a sandwich? We've got lots of leftover turkey."

They were in high spirits and discussed the wedding plans as they ate.

"I assure you that Peabody will be the joy of Wizzle's life in no time at all," promised Bruno as he and Boots climbed out over the sill. "Same here," said Cathy.

The two boys climbed down the drainpipe and jumped to the ground.

"Freeze!" came an earsplitting voice. Miss Peabody bounded onto the scene and was upon them in seconds. She grabbed them by their shirt collars and lifted them from the ground. "Aha! The troublemakers from Macdonald Hall! I'm going to make you sorry you showed up here tonight!" She turned her face upward. "Burton, Grant, is that you?"

"Yes," came Diane's small voice from above.

"No," Cathy called down. "We don't know who those two guys are. You woke us up, Miss Peabody."

"Balloonjuice!" bellowed the Assistant Headmistress. "Get your track shoes on and get down here! The four of you are going to run laps!"

"Laps?" echoed Bruno.

"Yes, laps. We're going to show you pampered babies from Macdonald Hall how discipline is enforced."

"But it's dark," protested Bruno.

"Don't worry. Burton knows the track." She looked up at the window. "Come on! Move it!"

Cathy and Diane disappeared for a while and then came out the front door to stand beside Bruno and Boots.

"Miss Peabody," said Cathy plaintively, "we ran laps all afternoon."

"And you're going to run laps all night! All right, you four, *move!*"

* * *

Mr. Sturgeon and his wife were driving home from the city late that night after spending the evening with Mrs. Sturgeon's sister and her family.

"Mildred," grumbled the Headmaster, "the next time we go visiting your relatives remind me to take my earplugs. Your brother-in-law didn't shut up from the time we arrived until we left. Who cares about the ins and outs of the plumbing business?"

"I thought you did, dear. You listened raptly."

"I was asleep, Mildred. And the children and grandchildren are worse. You know I cannot bear being called Uncle Willie."

As he approached the driveway to Macdonald Hall, his headlights illuminated a number of figures on Miss Scrimmage's athletic field.

"William, what on earth — It's one o'clock in the morning!" Mrs. Sturgeon squinted in the darkness. "Four children — and two of them are boys!"

Mr. Sturgeon hit the brakes and the car screeched to a halt. He leapt out and hit the road running. Sailing over the orchard fence as if it did not exist, he ran onto the athletic field.

"Walton — O'Neal — come here this instant!"

Bruno and Boots ran over, panting. Miss Peabody stormed after them and they scrambled quickly to stand behind their headmaster.

"Sturgeon, this is my campus and I'm the boss here! No one interferes with my punishments!"

"Indeed," said Mr. Sturgeon icily. "These two are my students and no one punishes them but me."

"They were on my territory after hours," said Miss Peabody. "I'm seeing to it that they won't return. Come on, you two. Back to the track."

"Do not move a muscle," commanded Mr. Sturgeon.

"Miss Peabody, can we stop running now?" came Cathy's voice.

"No! Keep going!"

"Come along, boys," said Mr. Sturgeon coldly. "We're leaving."

Miss Peabody moved to block their way.

"Young woman, kindly remove yourself from my path."

"You have no right to come over and undermine my authority on my own ground!" said Miss Peabody angrily.

Mr. Sturgeon's face flamed red. "If you do not move out of my way, you will regret it, madam."

Miss Peabody grinned. "What are you going to do — sic your sissy Board of Directors on me?"

Mr. Sturgeon glared at her menacingly. "Suffice it to say, madam, that you are not the only person in this world who knows jiu-jitsu. Now stand aside." Mr. Sturgeon led the boys around her and headed for the highway.

* * *

"Gee, Mr. Sturgeon," said Bruno admiringly, "I didn't know you knew jiu-jitsu."

"Shhh, Walton. Keep walking."

When they reached the highway, the Headmaster turned to the boys. "Be in my office tomorrow morning at eight. We'll have this out once and for all."

Chapter 14

a man in love

"I suppose it will come as a great surprise to you," said Mr. Sturgeon sarcastically the next morning, "that Miss Scrimmage's school is off limits to the boys of Macdonald Hall."

Bruno and Boots dropped their heads a little to avoid the Headmaster's gaze.

"Boys, I want to know right now if that nocturnal escapade had anything to do with the late Committee."

Bruno brightened. "Oh, no, sir. It had nothing to do with The Committee. We disbanded that when you told us to." He did not feel it prudent to mention The Coalition at this time.

"Well," said Mr. Sturgeon, "thank goodness for small

mercies. I should think that you boys would know better than to go over there in view of the furor raised when Miss Scrimmage's student body paid us an unscheduled visit so recently. No doubt Miss Burton and Miss Grant figured in this in some way."

Bruno and Boots studied the floor.

Mr. Sturgeon stood up and began pacing. "You two have been called into this office a number of times in the very recent past. If you are called here again, I shall have no choice but to suspend both of you. Is that clear?"

"Yes, sir." It was barely a whisper.

"Fine. In addition, you are confined to your room after dinner until further notice. You are dismissed."

Bruno and Boots opened the door.

"*And stay away from Scrimmage's!*" shouted Mr. Sturgeon. It was out of his mouth before he could modulate his tone.

"Ah, Walton, O'Neal," said Mr. Wizzle. "I heard about your deplorable activities last night. Ten demerits each." He was shaking his head as he took out his notebook. "Walton — eighty demerits! Five hundred and fifty lines! O'Neal — three hundred lines from you. Now run along."

Mrs. Davis walked into the Headmaster's office. "Mr. Sturgeon, I've never heard you shout like that. What on earth could have happened?"

"I'm not sure exactly," said the Headmaster, still agitated, "but in extricating those two from their difficulties, I may have threatened a lady with physical violence!"

* * *

"Bruno," said Mark Davies in disgust, "if you get one more demerit, we in the Lines Department are going to resign from The Coalition, The Committee and everything else!"

Bruno grinned apologetically. "Okay, you guys, the first meeting of the Macdonald Hall Chapter of The Coalition Department Heads will come to order."

Boots moaned. "Not so loud, Bruno! If The Fish gets wind of The Coalition, we're cooked!"

"Don't worry," said Bruno. "I would like to explain the one and only aim of The Coalition — Operation Matrimony. We're going to take Wizzle and marry him off."

"Don't be silly," mumbled Wilbur, his mouth full of pizza. "Who'd be stupid enough or desperate enough to marry Wizzle?"

"Miss Gloria Peabody," announced Bruno grandly.

Chris Talbot choked.

Elmer Drimsdale looked perplexed. "I don't understand the logic. If they marry, how is it going to help us? They'll still be here, presenting a united front."

"Not quite," said Bruno. "If they're in love, then they're going to be paying all their attention to each other. That means they'll have less time to cook up miserable things for us. Then, of course, they're bound to take a long honeymoon. And if we really play it right, they'll go off together to start their own school. Larry told me he's heard Wizzle say that Macdonald Hall is only a jumping-off point in his career. With Peabody at his side, maybe it'll give him the confidence to take that big step. Then we'll be rid of both of them. Great plan, eh, guys?"

There was a stunned silence.

"Bruno," said Wilbur, "I've always suspected it, but now I'm sure — you're crazy!"

"Well," grinned Bruno, "if you're not interested, *Hacken,*

we can get someone else to help."

"I'll help," muttered Wilbur.

"Bruno," said Larry, "there are some things you can do and some things you can't. You just can't control how people are going to feel about each other."

"Sure we can — " began Bruno.

"Yeah," interrupted Boots sarcastically. "We're The Committee."

"The Coalition," corrected Bruno. "Now listen carefully. Here's what we're going to do . . . "

* * *

Mr. Wizzle was in his office preparing a memo to all staff on scheduling more psychological testing when Larry Wilson's voice wafted in through the half-open door.

"Boy, Bruno, I wish I was at Scrimmage's! I could just sit and look at her all day!"

Mr. Wizzle looked up from his memo.

"I know what you mean," came Bruno's voice. "Miss Peabody sure is gorgeous. I wish I was Mr. Wizzle."

Larry sighed. "Yeah, she's sweet on him all right. And he doesn't even seem to know it."

"Oh, I'll bet he knows it," said Bruno. "He's just playing it cool."

Larry sighed again. "Gee, she's beautiful!"

Inside the office, Mr. Wizzle stared perplexedly at the crack in the doorway. Miss Peabody was sweet on him?

* * *

Miss Peabody was walking down the hall of the dormitory when Diane Grant's voice reached her from around a corner. ". . . and with those glasses, he's just so cute!"

"Oh, I know!" squealed the voice of Cathy Burton. "I

dreamed about Mr. Wizzle last night. I was held prisoner in this castle and he programmed the computer to slay the dragon and get me out. He's adorable!"

"But he's too old for any of us," lamented Diane. "Besides, anybody can see he's crazy about Miss Peabody."

"And she's playing hard-to-get," added Cathy.

"Boy, if it were me, I'd grab him in a minute. He's so —"

"All right, you!" roared Miss Peabody, swooping down on them from around the corner. "Why aren't you doing your homework?"

"Oh, we finished it, Miss Peabody," said Cathy. "We were just doing a little — wishful thinking."

"Well, don't," snapped Miss Peabody. "Get back to your room or I'll have you both running the track."

The girls scurried off.

Miss Peabody stood for a moment, frowning. Wizzle was crazy about her? Since when?

* * *

Alex Flynn, athletic director of Macdonald Hall, was rummaging through the equipment room. He had decided to start the senior phys. ed. classes on a program of Manchurian toe-ball, but he couldn't find any wickets. He was just making a mental note to order some when he came across a gigantic brown bag behind a stack of mats. It was tied shut with twine, and on it was scribbled *Wizzle*.

Flynn snorted in annoyance. If this belonged to Wizzle, what was it doing cluttering up his equipment room? He picked the heavy package up, left the gymnasium and began walking across the campus to Mr. Wizzle's cottage.

There was no answer to his knock. He turned and looked back towards the Faculty Building. There were still lights on. Wizzle was probably working late on his latest software innovation. Flynn tried the door. It was unlocked. He deposited the bulky package on the bottom shelf of Wizzle's hall table and left the house, shutting the door behind him.

As he walked back across the campus towards the gym, all thoughts of Mr. Wizzle's parcel left his mind. Now, where was he going to get those wickets . . .

* * *

It was almost lights-out when Bruno and Boots answered the knocking at their door. Chris and Elmer stood there, chalk-white and trembling.

"Hi, Chris, Elm. What's the matter?"

"Bruno!" gasped Chris. "The balloon! It's — "

"Oh, the balloon," Bruno interrupted. "That was strictly a Committee thing. The Coalition doesn't need it. I'm sorry about all your hard work."

"Bruno, listen to me!" Chris insisted. "The balloon is gone! It's disappeared!"

"What do you mean, 'disappeared?'" squeaked Boots. "Where is it?"

"We don't know!"

"It was in the equipment room of the gym," explained Elmer, "behind some mats. It was there yesterday, but today it's gone."

"Was it finished?" asked Bruno.

"Almost," said Elmer. "Chris finished the painting and tonight we were going to connect the remote control to the inflater."

Boots brightened. "What a relief! Then it won't go off!"

"Not exactly," said Elmer. "If roughly handled, it could accidentally inflate."

"You mean," finished Boots, all the colour draining from his face, "that any minute now, from we-don't-know-where, a ten-metre Wizzle balloon might suddenly whoosh into being in the middle of the campus?"

Bruno grinned. "Boy, would that ever be funny!"

"No it wouldn't," said Boots positively. "We're not allowed to bug Mr. Wizzle, and if a ten-metre balloon isn't bugging him, I don't know what is! Bruno, The Fish is going to kill us!"

"Don't worry," soothed Bruno. "It hasn't happened yet. And it'll probably never happen."

"But where is it?" moaned Chris. "It didn't just walk away! What could have happened to it?"

"It doesn't matter," said Bruno. "It's a Committee balloon, and as members of The Coalition, we don't have to worry about it. We're just going to ignore it and continue convincing Wizzle that Peabody's gorgeous. So why don't you guys go to your rooms and get a good night's sleep. It's after lights-out."

Unconvinced, Chris and Elmer straggled off.

"Bruno," said Boots, "you know The Fish has threatened us with suspension. If that balloon floats up from somewhere, we'll be blamed for it. We'll be lucky if we're just suspended. Expelled would be more like it. Probably shot, too. Bruno, I love being at Macdonald Hall. Macdonald Hall with Wizzle is better than no Macdonald Hall at all. And also, my folks would kill me."

"Really, Boots," said Bruno earnestly, "there's nothing

to worry about. Pretty soon Wizzle and Peabody will be married and a thing of the past. And then it won't matter if the balloon turns up because no one will be offended. The Fish will just laugh it off when we explain that it was all built way back before he ordered us to disband The Committee. So let's just go to bed and forget about the whole thing."

Bruno and Boots got into their pajamas and climbed into bed. Boots glanced over at the remote control button for Elmer's low-frequency sound generator. "At least we haven't been giving Wizzle any earthquakes recently."

"Of course not," said Bruno. "A man in love needs his sleep."

* * *

Miss Scrimmage and Miss Peabody sat in the sitting room. The Headmistress poured two cups of tea from her very best china pot and faced her assistant with some trepidation.

"Now, what was it you wanted to see me about?" asked Miss Peabody, downing the entire cup and looking her employer squarely in the eye.

"Oh dear," said Miss Scrimmage uncomfortably. "This is so delicate. For the last week or so, a large number of the girls have been speaking to me — lady to lady — "

"What do you mean?" asked Miss Peabody impatiently. "Don't tell me they're complaining about me again. I'll soon run that out of them."

"No, no," said Miss Scrimmage. "It seems that the girls are — well — enamoured — of young Mr. Wizzle from Macdonald Hall. And they are all heartsick because — uh — they say — er — they say he's in love with another woman — and that she's you." Miss Scrimmage finished in a rush, pink to the roots of her hair.

"Balloonjuice!" exploded Miss Peabody. "The girls can't be in love with Wizzle. He's — dull and pudgy."

"Nonetheless, they are," said Miss Scrimmage. "And I felt that I should bring it to your attention. They seemed quite definite about Mr. Wizzle's — er — regard for you."

"That's even more balloonjuice! Where would they get such a stupid idea? Wizzle and I hardly ever see each other, and when we do we fight. Don't worry, Miss Scrimmage. A few laps of the track will run this out of their systems."

"Now, Miss Peabody," Miss Scrimmage went on, "you must realize that the girls are a little angry with you. They feel you've been trifling with the affections of their — ahem — sweetheart."

"This is ridiculous!" exclaimed Miss Peabody. "They need exercise!" She stormed out of the sitting room.

* * *

Mr. Wizzle sat at his desk, staring out the window at an oak tree on which someone had carved a large heart enclosing the initials W.W. and G.P. The campus was covered with this graffiti. For more than a week now he had been overhearing his name linked romantically with Miss Peabody's. And Miss Peabody was enjoying incredible popularity at Macdonald Hall. Her name was scribbled on notebooks; boys talked about her with love in their eyes; the more artistic students sketched her; why, one boy had even handed in his punishment lines with a love sonnet to her written on the back. The boys were looking at him with envy as the man who had captured her heart.

Had he? And why all this admiration? Miss Peabody was a lovely girl, but surely — Perhaps he hadn't looked clearly enough. Well, he would call her, just to chat.

He picked up the phone and dialled Miss Scrimmage's number.

"Ah, yes — Miss Peabody, please . . . Uh, hello there. This is Walter . . . Wizzle. Walter Wizzle . . . Ah, yes. Hello . . . Why I called? Uh — well — I just wanted to inquire as to — how things are going . . . Oh, that's good. Everything is fine here, too . . . Yes, good-bye, Miss Peabody."

He hung up the phone and looked off into space. She didn't *seem* to be in love with him. In fact, she had sounded somewhat standoffish — indifferent even. A goofy grin spread over his face. She was shy!

Miss Peabody sat at her desk, her arms folded and cradling her head, staring across the room at a large poster of a tank she had on the wall.

For the past three days Wizzle had been phoning intermittently and even showing up at the school asking if there was anything he could do to help out. It was creating havoc among the girls, who honestly did seem to idolize the man (though for what reason she could not possibly imagine). But why was he hanging around? Could he actually be seeking out her company? The girls seemed to think so. Miss Scrimmage was sure of it and had assumed the role of motherly chaperone, inviting Wizzle for hundreds of cups of tea. It was all a load of balloon-juice, and yet . . .

* * *

Bruno and Boots helped Cathy and Diane in through their window.

"Sorry we couldn't come over to you," said Bruno, "but things have been pretty heavy with The Fish lately and we couldn't risk it."

"Oh, that's okay," smiled Cathy. "We just came over for a Coalition meeting. How are the wedding plans?"

"Great," grinned Bruno. "I think Wizzle's falling in love. He's over visiting Peabody practically every day. They'll probably get married soon."

Boots laughed. "Bruno, people don't get married just because you want them to. It'll take a little more time than that if it ever happens at all."

"Really?" asked Bruno. "How long?"

Diane shrugged. "Months. Years."

"No!" Bruno was aghast. "We can't wait that long. We'll have to figure out some way to speed up the process."

"Well, Miss Scrimmage is on our side," said Cathy. "She's fawning all over them and playing mother of the bride. The only thing that bothers me is Peabody. Who can tell what she's feeling? That is, if she's feeling anything at all. How can we melt her heart if she doesn't have a heart to melt?"

"Hmmm," said Bruno. "How about — yeah! Send her some flowers and candy and stuff like that and say it's from Wizzle!"

Diane was unconvinced. "She'd probably be charmed more by an M-16 rifle."

"Don't be so negative," said Cathy. "Okay, we'll look after the flowers and candy. Let's go. See you, guys."

"Bruno," said Boots after the girls had left, "this is all crazy. It's never going to work. And if The Fish gets wind of it — We ought to stop it."

"It's not so simple," said Bruno. "We made Wizzle fall in love with Peabody. Now we have a moral responsibility to see to it that she loves him back."

Boots did not reply. He was having a giddy vision of a ten-metre Wizzle balloon rising out of nowhere in front of Mr. Sturgeon.

* * *

Well, thought Miss Peabody, alone in Miss Scrimmage's sitting room, there wasn't any doubt about it. Wizzle was in love with her all right. This morning a huge bouquet of flowers had appeared outside her door. There had been no card, but it was obviously Wizzle's doing. And at Miss Scrimmage's endless teas he did nothing but compliment her on her hair, her eyes, her clothes, even her shoes.

Why her?

"Oh, look!" came Miss Scrimmage's voice from the hall. Miss Peabody mouthed the words along with the Headmistress's now daily ritual. "Look who's here. It's Mr. Wizzle. Do come in and have some tea, won't you'"

Mr. Wizzle bounced energetically into the room and beamed at Miss Peabody.

"Hello, Wizzle," she said without enthusiasm. Miss Scrimmage sat down and began clinking teacups.

"It's a beautiful day," commented Mr. Wizzle. It was a poetic remark brought on by the nearness of Miss Peabody.

Miss Peabody sighed. "Thanks for the flowers, Wizzle."

He was taken aback. She had received flowers! But he had sent no flowers! A crushing thought occurred to him. There was another man. Someone else had noticed Miss Peabody and sent her flowers. Who could it be? Sturgeon?

No, too old, and married besides. Fudge? No, not Fudge. Flynn? Of course! Coach Flynn was after Miss Peabody!

"Is something wrong, Mr. Wizzle?" asked Miss Scrimmage in concern. "You look rather pale."

"No, no, everything's fine," replied Mr. Wizzle with false heartiness. "It's just that I can't stay very long today. I've got to do some shopping."

He would buy presents for Miss Peabody — beautiful presents, lots of them. And he would start exercising regularly until he had trimmed down a little.

Chapter 15

la montagne

"Quilting!" Mr. Sturgeon slapped the letters joyously onto the Scrabble board. "Now let's see. That's fifty points for using all the letters — eighteen points times three for the triple word score — that's fifty-four — and seven points for joining the *g* to *asp* — a hundred and eleven all told, Mildred. I'm killing you this game!" He grinned with satisfaction.

His wife smiled. "I haven't seen you this happy in a long time, William. Surely it can't be just because you're winning the game."

Mr. Sturgeon chortled happily. "I'm Headmaster again, Mildred. For the past couple of weeks Wizzle's been spending so much time over at Scrimmage's that he's hardly ever here. It's wonderful."

"At Scrimmage's? Why does he go there?"

"Mildred, haven't you heard? He's courting Miss Peabody."

"Really?" Mrs. Sturgeon clasped her hands. "How lovely!"

"It certainly is. We haven't heard the clattering of that computer for more than a week."

"You mean he's neglecting his duties?"

"Fortunately, yes," said the Headmaster, "and everyone's better off for it. He really seems to have fallen for her. He's constantly carrying presents and flowers and candy over to her, and he's even taken up jogging along the road in front of Scrimmage's every morning!"

"And does Miss Peabody return his affection?"

"I devoutly hope so," said the Headmaster. "If she does not, then your Mr. Wizzle is making a perfect ninnyhammer out of himself. Come on, Mildred. It's your turn."

* * *

"I don't understand what's taking so long!" complained Bruno. "Why aren't they married yet? It's been almost a month!"

"The problem is Peabody," said Cathy. "She's got no heart. Are you absolutely sure there's no such thing as a love potion?"

"Positive," said Bruno. "Hmmm. Maybe it's not all Peabody. Maybe it's Wizzle. He's just not forceful enough. Girls, what do they do when they're together at Scrimmage's?"

"Nothing," said Diane. "They have tea with Miss Scrimmage."

"Well, that's the problem!" exclaimed Bruno. "I think we're going to have to work on Wizzle's confidence so he'll ask her for a date and they can be alone together."

"How are we going to do that?" asked Boots.

Bruno grinned. "You'll see."

* * *

Mr. Wizzle was sitting at his desk gift-wrapping a volume of war poetry when the voices of Bruno Walton and Boots O'Neal wafted in through the open window.

"My brother wrote me a letter," Bruno was saying. "He wants to get to know this girl, but he doesn't know how to approach her and he wanted my advice. At first I didn't know what to tell him and then I thought 'What would Mr. Wizzle do?' After that it was all clear to me."

Boots whistled. "Yeah, that Mr. Wizzle sure has a way with women."

"I know," said Bruno. "Take Miss Peabody, for instance. He knows that she's the type of woman who appreciates forcefulness. I'll bet he doesn't waste time beating around the bush. He'd just step right in there and ask her out, straight as an arrow!"

Mr. Wizzle sat taller in his chair. Yes! That was exactly what he would do!

* * *

"Hello, Peabody speaking . . . Oh, Wizzle, it's you . . . Friday night? . . . Are you sure you really want that? . . . Well — uh — okay, I guess so. Good-bye, Wizzle."

Miss Peabody slammed down the receiver with an annoyed frown. Now, why had she accepted his invitation? What a waste of a Friday night! Why would someone who had no trouble at all kicking three hundred butts into shape not have the guts to tell Wizzle that she didn't want to go out with him on Friday evening? Surely a former U.S. Marine could manage to say, "No, Wizzle, I don't want to go out with you." Of course. Then why hadn't she said it?

Oh, well, with any luck Friday would go badly and even Wizzle would be able to see that the two of them were just not compatible. Reassured by this thought, she resumed her paper work.

* * *

Late Friday night Miss Scrimmage stood in the doorway of the residence hall to welcome Miss Peabody home from her date.

"Hello, dear. How was your evening?"

"Terrible!" muttered Miss Peabody, trudging into the building. "Just don't ask!"

Miss Scrimmage was aghast. "Did Mr. Wizzle make improper advances?"

The Assistant Headmistress rolled her eyes. "Do you know what his idea of a big time is? We went to a cello recital!"

"Oh, how nice."

"I yawned so wide I thought he'd fall in! Anyway, I don't want to talk about it. Good night."

She walked to her room, reflecting that the worst part of the whole dreary experience was that she couldn't bring herself to tell Wizzle that they were through. She entered her room and kicked her Niagara Falls cushion, another gift from Wizzle, across the floor. Why should she feel obliged to tell Wizzle they were finished when they had never even started?

"He's a dead loss, that's what he is. A dead loss," said Bruno glumly at the lunch table. "He stinks with women. Boots and I were talking with Cathy. Wizzle took Peabody out Friday night. You know where he took her? A cello recital! You know — those big violins that moan a lot. I just can't believe it! At this rate it'll be years before they even hold hands!"

"It's hopeless," said Boots. "They're the least romantic pair in the world."

"It does seem unlikely that we will achieve our goal of matrimony," put in Elmer.

"You guys are just going about it the wrong way," said Wilbur.

"Oh, yeah?" challenged Bruno. "Since when did you become the big Casanova?"

"It's very simple," Wilbur insisted. "There's only one thing you should use to get two people in the mood to grow fond of each other."

"What's that?" asked Boots.

"Food."

Everyone laughed.

"No, really!" said Wilbur, now so involved in the argument that he was ignoring his lunch. "Think about it. When families get together they put on a big spread; when married couples celebrate their anniversaries they have supper together; when major corporations form business affiliations the contract is signed in a restaurant over lunch; and when two people are interested in each other they have intimate dinners by candlelight." He looked around. "Right?"

There were still snickers.

"No. No — wait!" said Bruno. "He's got a point there. Let's set Wizzle and Peabody up for a romantic dinner. Now let's see — where?"

"Ralph's Diner has the best hamburgers in Chutney," offered Pete Anderson.

"No, no," said Sidney. "It's got to be classier than that. Maybe fish and chips."

"No," said Bruno. "It's got to be somewhere really nice."

"My uncle Manfred owns a restaurant," said Wilbur.

"What's it called?!" grinned Larry. "Mr. Eat?"

Wilbur looked insulted. "Have you ever heard of Manny's?"

"*The* Manny's?" Chris goggled. "That fancy place in downtown Toronto?"

Wilbur nodded proudly. "Food is a serious business in our family. Last year the president of the United States dined there on his trip to Toronto. It's got a five-star rating."

Bruno smiled broadly. "That settles it. Saturday night Wizzle and Peabody are going out for the most fantastic dinner of their lives."

Boots frowned. "Bruno, if this Manny's is as fancy as Wilbur says it is, it's going to cost a fortune."

"So what?" shrugged Bruno. "Wizzle's paying. Wilbur, make the reservation. Ask your uncle for the best table."

* * *

Mr. Wizzle walked into his office to find a mauve envelope on his desk. He opened it and removed a perfumed note in elegant, flowing handwriting. It read simply: *Manny's, Saturday night, eight o'clock.*

He held the note to his nose and inhaled the deep scent of lavender. His heart soared. Miss Peabody was meeting him for dinner!

Miss Peabody read the note she found on her desk. It was printed quite professionally on a white sheet of paper. *Miss Gloria Peabody, Please meet with me at Manny's in downtown Toronto on Saturday at exactly eight o'clock. This may seriously concern your future. A Friend.*

She frowned. Wizzle? No, it couldn't be. It had too much style. Who could it be then? What could it mean? The tone of the letter was vaguely threatening. She set her jaw stubbornly. Well, she would definitely get to the bottom of this — on Saturday at eight.

* * *

"Right on time, half an hour early," announced Bruno triumphantly. He, Boots and Wilbur sat in the waiters' room off the gleaming kitchen of Manny's renowned restaurant. They watched the closed-circuit TV screen as Wilbur's uncle personally escorted Mr. Wizzle to a private dining room.

"This TV thing is great!" exclaimed Bruno gleefully. "This way you can spy on all the people eating here!"

"It's not for spying," said Wilbur indignantly. "It's so waiters can watch their tables without hovering around the people."

"Yeah, well, it's a really fancy place," said Bruno. "I'm glad your uncle's nice enough to let us in here."

Boots looked at his watch. "I wonder how long it'll be before Peabody arrives. I'd like to get this over with and get back to school before The Fish finds out we're gone. We're supposed to be confined to our room, you know."

"Relax," said Wilbur. "Uncle Manfred's garlic bread is worth any risk. Have some."

Bruno and Boots each took a piece of bread and continued to watch the screen. Just then Wilbur's Uncle Manfred came up behind them. "Well, gentlemen, everything is ready except for the wine. Any suggestions?"

"Wine?" asked Bruno uncertainly.

"Of course," replied the restaurateur. "We always serve a complimentary bottle with our private dinners. Since you know the happy couple, I thought you might recommend something . . . "

"Well," Bruno said, "what kind of wine would you serve at a wedding?"

"Champagne, naturally."

Bruno nodded. "If you say so, then champagne it is."

The boys went back to watching the screen.

On the stroke of eight o'clock, Miss Peabody appeared at the front entrance.

"This is it!" exclaimed Bruno. He turned to the employee in charge of piping background music into the restaurant. "Remember — when she walks into the room, play that song."

Manfred Hackenschleimer escorted Miss Peabody to the private dining room and bowed her inside.

"Miss Peabody!" said Mr. Wizzle, leaping to his feet as violin music swelled through the room.

She stared at him. "Wizzle. It's you."

"Yes, well, here we are."

Miss Peabody took an involuntary step into the room, knowing full well that she should have been taking a voluntary step out of it. Well, she wasn't staying, that was all. She would just stay long enough not to hurt his feelings, and then she would put an end to this once and for all.

Cautiously she sat down. "Wizzle, I — "

A waiter walked discreetly into the room. "Ah, Mr. Wizzle and Miss Peabody. Good evening. I am Maurice." He placed a large silver ice bucket on a stand beside the table. "Champagne, compliments of the house."

"Er — that's very nice," said Mr. Wizzle.

Glad of the interruption, Miss Peabody nodded in agreement.

Skillfully Maurice opened the champagne and poured a small amount into Mr. Wizzle's glass for his approval.

Mr. Wizzle tasted the champagne and pronounced it worthy, secretly hoping that it was. As a non-drinker, he had no conception of what differentiated good champagne from bad. Maurice withdrew silently.

"A toast to you, Miss Peabody," said Mr. Wizzle, beaming.

Geez, thought Miss Peabody, and drained her glass.

He refilled it. She drank deeply again. This was not working out. How could she tell Wizzle she was leaving?

"You look beautiful!" he blurted, and gulped some champagne.

Miss Peabody was at a loss for words. Wizzle was a wimp, but the dark suit he was wearing tonight gave him an almost military appearance. And all that furious jogging she had prescribed was beginning to pay off . . . She picked up her glass and drained it again, conscious that she was blushing. This was ridiculous — U.S. Marines did not blush. Get a hold of yourself, she thought. After all, this was the man who had taken her to a cello recital.

"Look, Wizzle — "

Maurice peered in again. "Ah, enjoying your champagne, I see. Would you care to order?"

"Certainly." Mr. Wizzle looked questioningly at Miss Peabody.

But she was just leaving . . . "Uh — I'll have the Boeuf Charlemagne, please." It looked as if she would have to eat dinner with him.

Bruno was staring at the screen. "I can't tell what's going on! Are they having a good time?"

Boots shrugged. "How should I know? I wish they'd hurry it up."

"Fine dining is never hurried," explained Wilbur, who was watching some of the other tables with great interest. "Now, the man in the blue suit at table fourteen really knows his food. He's having the duck à l'orange with white wine."

Maurice came into the waiters' room.

"What did they order?" asked Wilbur excitedly. "Boeuf Charlemagne for the lady, and for the gentleman, Caesar salad."

"Hey, don't put too much garlic in Wizzle's salad," cautioned Bruno. "If he's got bad breath, Peabody won't marry him."

Maurice drew himself up in a huff. "Our chef always uses exactly the right amount of everything!"

Mr. Wizzle eyed his paté de foie gras suspiciously. He was a vegetarian, and this looked a lot like meat. But Miss Peabody was having hers, so he would have to eat it to make a good impression.

Miss Peabody looked at him sharply. "I thought you didn't eat meat, Wizzle."

"Uh — I don't, but — I mean, this is a special occasion."

Miss Peabody thought back to the note that had summoned her here. *This may seriously concern your future,* it had said. Oh, no! She grabbed her glass, drained it, filled it up again and drank a bit more until all thoughts of the note were gone from her mind.

In the waiters' room Bruno beckoned to Maurice. "They've almost finished the champagne. Could you bring them another bottle?"

"Certainly," said Maurice. "Is this also to be compliments of the house?"

Bruno checked The Coalition treasury, presently residing in his wallet. "No," he sighed. "I think Wizzle will have to pay for this one."

Maurice walked into the kitchen.

"What's going on?" asked Boots nervously.

"Well, they're waiting for their dinner and having some more champagne," said Bruno. "I can't tell if they like each other, though. Wizzle looks as if he likes her, but she looks kind of strange."

"Wait till she tastes the Boeuf Charlemagne," said Wilbur confidently. "What a sauce!"

Mr. Wizzle took another drink of champagne. He found it gave him courage. "I'm very glad that we could be here together tonight, Miss Peabody," he ventured boldly.

Immediately she reached for her glass. Well, this was a fine state of affairs. The more charming Wizzle tried to be, the more she drank. Why didn't she just tell him and go home?

Maurice slithered into the room. "More champagne, sir?"

"Good idea!" she said before he could answer.

Bruno kept on monitoring the room, Boots had a nervous eye on the clock, and Wilbur watched a waiter skillfully flame desserts at various tables. The minutes ticked away as Mr. Wizzle and Miss Peabody were served.

At last Maurice spirited away the dishes and the two diners sat at the table finishing the champagne. Miss Peabody's thoughts were in turmoil. She was reasonably certain that she was disgusted with herself, but she could not seem to remember why. She looked across the table into Mr. Wizzle's big, earnest and slightly glazed eyes. A low giggling sound began in her throat.

He looked at her. "Miss Peabody, is something the matter?"

She focused on his face. "Wizzle, you're a perfect gentleman," she said and then broke into hysterical laughter.

He looked at her uncertainly. "Miss Peabody, you're a perfect lady."

This struck her as even funnier, and she put her head down on the table for support as her laughter swelled again.

A smile cracked Mr. Wizzle's confused face. He was not sure what was happening, but whatever it was it must be — laughable. That was enough for him. He cracked up, too.

In the waiters' room Bruno's eyes bulged. "*Hey!* They're smiling! They're laughing! They must be in love! Wilbur, you're a genius!"

The three boys crowded around the screen.

"I wouldn't call that love," said Boots dryly. "I'd call that crazy."

"We did it!" cheered Bruno.

Maurice came into the room.

"Did they order dessert?" asked Wilbur in suspense.

The waiter nodded. "They're having La Montagne."

Wilbur's jaw dropped. "Ooh! La Montagne!"

Boots looked at him. "What's that?"

"It's chocolate and cream and nuts and cherries and brandy — and it's the best-tasting thing in the whole world! I want some!"

Maurice smiled and went into the kitchen.

"I think we should go home," said Boots. "They're in love, so now we can split."

"Everything has to be perfect," said Bruno. "We're staying here every minute to make sure they have the best time of their lives. Look! They're smiling and chatting just like people! You know, when Miss Peabody smiles, she's not half-ugly!"

"I'm going to ask Uncle Manfred if there's any leftover La Montagne!" Wilbur rushed out.

"We can't stay very late," Boots insisted.

Bruno could smell victory within his grasp. "Patience, Melvin."

By midnight Miss Peabody and Mr. Wizzle had finished their dessert as well as numerous liqueurs with their coffee.

"Wizzle," said Miss Peabody, her words considerably slurred, "do you realize that I didn't want to stay here with you?"

"No," he said, laughing foolishly.

"I wonder why I wanted to go home," she said thoughtfully. "Scrimmage doesn't serve La Montagne."

"Maybe there was a fight on TV," he suggested.

"I hate TV."

"Me too."

"I like fighting, though."

"I noticed."

By this time Boots was frantic. "Bruno, Wilbur, let's go! They could sit here for hours!"

Even Bruno was concerned. "You know, they look kind of strange. I mean, it's okay to laugh and have a good time, but they're all red and leaning all over the place and they look — weird. I wonder what's the matter."

Maurice supplied the answer. "I'll tell you what's the matter. Monsieur and Mademoiselle are very, very drunk. I trust that you have arranged to escort them home, as they are on the verge of — shall we say — passing out."

"But they're our teachers!" protested Boots in horror. "They'll recognize us!"

"My dear fellow," said Maurice, "I can assure you that, in their present state, those two young people would not recognize their own mothers."

Bruno took out his wallet and checked The Coalition treasury. "We've got just enough for a taxi. I hope Wizzle's got enough for the bill. Come on — let's go collect them."

As the loaded taxi made its way north along Highway 48 to Macdonald Hall and Miss Scrimmage's, out the open window wafted the singing voices of Miss Peabody and Mr. Wizzle: "*It's a long way to Tipperary . . .* "

Chapter 16

the odd couple

Mr. Wizzle was walking across the campus the next morning wondering why his head ached so abominably. He squinted into the sunlight. A large group of boys, led by Bruno Walton, was bearing down on him.

"Hey, Mr. Wizzle!" shouted Bruno. "Congratulations!"

The boys swarmed around him, shaking his hand and patting him on the back and arms.

"Gee, Mr. Wizzle, that's great!"

"Congratulations!"

"You must be a very happy man!"

"What are you boys talking about?" Mr. Wizzle asked when the uproar had finally died down a little.

"We heard the good news!" exclaimed Bruno. "It's just

been announced across the road that you proposed to Miss Peabody last night — and she accepted!"

A large chorus of cheers went up from the crowd.

Mr. Wizzle gasped. He did? She did? Most of last night was just a blur to him, but how could he have forgotten something so important?

"Uh, thank you very much, boys," he stammered, and took off on the run for his house.

Desperately he tried to recall what had occurred last night, but he drew a blank. All he could remember was waking up at home in the morning, fully dressed, with all the money in his wallet gone. Had he been robbed?

Darting into the guest cottage, he began to pace the living room. He *should* remember doing something that would affect his life so drastically! Everything was so unclear!

Suddenly his head snapped up. Why was he standing here thinking cold, calculating thoughts? He was engaged to be married to the most wonderful woman in the world! He jumped up and danced a little jig, setting off a jackhammer in his head. Well, nothing could spoil his day today. The whole world was bright and beautiful, and even going for an aspirin would be a wonderful experience.

* * *

Miss Peabody was walking through the hall of the dormitory on her way to the infirmary for something to settle her stomach when she came face to face with Cathy Burton and a delegation of girls.

"Here she is," announced Cathy. "Here's the bride!"

The Assistant Headmistress looked at her menacingly.

"Burton, I'm in no mood for your nonsense. You wouldn't believe how many laps I can assign when I'm feeling like this."

"But we just heard the news!" insisted Cathy.

"What news?"

"That Mr. Wizzle popped the question last night and you accepted! Oh, we're all so happy for you!" The girls began to sing "Here Comes the Bride."

"Cut the noise!" barked Miss Peabody. Nonchalantly she strolled back to her room, let herself in and shut the door. Once inside, she collapsed onto her bed.

Oh, no! What had she done? Sometime in the midst of all that fantastic food and great champagne she had agreed to marry Wizzle! Now what was she going to do?

Outside the door stood Cathy and Diane, leaning and listening.

"Do you think she's going to buy it?" whispered Diane.

"I don't know," said Cathy nervously. "I can't hear anything."

"Well, she didn't exactly jump for joy when we told her," said Diane. "I think she'll call it off."

"If she does," promised Cathy, "I'll kill myself!"

The girls waited outside for the better part of an hour and then went for breakfast.

Inside, Miss Peabody's thoughts were still in a turmoil. If only she'd had the strength to hang up on him when he'd called, to kick him back across the highway when he'd come visiting, to refuse his presents, to say no when he'd offered to take her out — it was all her own weakness.

But that was impossible. She was a U.S. Marine. There

was no such thing as weakness. If she hadn't said no to Wizzle, it was because she hadn't wanted to!

Right! She was in love with the man!

Granted, he did have a few faults. Granted, he was still a little soft and pudgy. But that only added to the challenge. She could whip Wizzle into shape in six months — a year at the outside. When she got through with him, he'd be the perfect man.

And the girls were right. He did look kind of cute behind those glasses.

* * *

Wedding fever hit Macdonald Hall and Miss Scrimmage's. The big date was set and Miss Scrimmage's sewing classes thrust themselves heart and soul into the task of making Miss Peabody's wedding dress. Miss Scrimmage and the girls held a bridal tea, and Bruno and Boots got together with Coach Flynn and Mr. Fudge and threw a bachelor dinner. The Coalition set itself the task of raising money for a spectacular wedding gift, and students from both schools were giving from the heart.

The happiest person of all was definitely Miss Scrimmage. She had not had very much say in the running of her school during Miss Peabody's regime, and the wedding offered her a fantastic opportunity to take charge of the situation. She had always felt that her young ladies were being groomed for just such social undertakings, and the planning and execution of a wedding seemed heaven sent.

The engaged couple went along much as before, having afternoon tea with Miss Scrimmage, the occasional dinner with the Sturgeons and long walks together in the evenings. Mr. Wizzle sang a lot, and Miss Peabody smiled a little more when she assigned laps. The two had asked to be released from their contracts so that they could start work on a blueprint for their own school, which they planned to open the next fall. This pleased Miss Scrimmage, Mr. Sturgeon and, definitely, The Coalition.

Mr. Sturgeon viewed the whole thing with a feeling of unreality. He voiced it to his wife one morning after breakfast.

"Can you believe, Mildred, that in less than one week's time Wizzle and Peabody will be married on the south lawn of our campus, weather permitting?"

"I'm so happy for those two young people," she smiled. "Young love is so sweet."

The Headmaster chuckled over his toast. "I wish I knew how that unlikely union came to pass. There is certainly no accounting for the taste of some people."

"Now, William, that's unkind. Oh, I'm so looking forward to the wedding."

"I'm not," said the Headmaster. "Miss Scrimmage wouldn't let me hire a caterer. Her girls are doing the whole affair. Do you know what that means? We're having Scrim-food, Mildred — Scrim-cakes, Scrim-punch and Scrim-wiches. My stomach may never be the same."

"I'm sure it will be very nice," Mrs. Sturgeon said stoutly.

"We'll see," he replied skeptically. "Anyway, I don't think anyone will be as happy as our students. They've been trying to get rid of Wizzle since day one."

"William, I expect you to be perfectly charming at the wedding. After all, you're the host. And you are giving the bride away."

"*What?*" Mr. Sturgeon tipped over the jar of grape jelly. "Under no circumstances — "

"Oh, didn't I mention that, dear? Miss Scrimmage and I thought it would be a nice idea."

"But, Mildred, Miss Peabody and I are not on good terms!"

"Oh, that's all forgotten, William. This is a wedding."

"Oh, all right," he grumbled. "I wonder who's going to give Wizzle away. Walton, probably." He chuckled.

"Now, dear — "

* * *

The big day dawned warm and sunny. The ceremony was scheduled for 3:30, so the girls spent the morning busily arranging flowers and decorations at the site, right in front of Mr. Wizzle's cottage. Some of the boys had already started setting up long rows of folding chairs on either side of the red carpet that was to be the bridal aisle.

Mr. Wizzle, however, was not in his cottage to witness the flurry of activity for his wedding. At seven o'clock that morning he had appeared on the Sturgeons' doorstep, a foolish grin on his face, eyes red from lack of sleep, completely dressed in his striped trousers, cutaway coat and boutonniere. Mrs. Sturgeon had fed him breakfast and listened to his nervous, ecstatic babbling with compassion. When he showed no signs of leaving, Mr. Sturgeon had summoned Coach Flynn, the best man, and entrusted Wizzle to his care.

"What am I going to do with him?" Flynn had asked in bewilderment.

"That's entirely up to you. Perhaps a movie or two. Just

see to it that he's away from here until it's time for the wedding."

Even Bruno Walton was up early on the momentous day.

"This afternoon's the one time I'm not going to complain about wearing a tie," he announced, rubbing his hands together in glee. "Just think — in less than twelve hours Wizzle and Peabody will be on their honeymoon and we'll never have to worry again!"

Boots was nervous. "Bruno, I don't know about all this. Maybe Mr. Wizzle and Miss Peabody aren't getting married because they want to — they may be getting married because The Coalition set them up. And that would be wrong."

"No way," said Bruno with firm conviction. "We wouldn't have paired them off it they weren't perfect for each other."

"Yeah, but — "

"Look," said Bruno, "there are only two things that are important here — Wizzle's happy and *I'm* happy. Have you ever seen me so happy?"

Boots laughed. "You're impossible, you know that?" He threw a calculus textbook, but Bruno ducked. The book struck a shelf, bringing down half a dozen other books onto the bureau and floor. Grinning, Boots moved to pick them up.

"Forget it," laughed Bruno, grabbing his roommate by the arm and leading him out the door. "Let's go help them set up the chairs."

They slammed the door behind them. On the bureau a heavy physics text slipped and came to rest on top of the remote control button of Elmer's earthquake machine.

Across the campus the empty guest cottage began to vibrate silently.

* * *

At exactly half past three that afternoon, under a brightly shining sun and clear blue sky, Miss Scrimmage's top music student began the opening chords of the Wedding March.

Down the red carpet came Miss Peabody on the arm of Mr. Sturgeon. Her gown was satin and lace, gleaming richly in the brightness of the day. She had refused to wear the veil, dismissing it as stupid and useless, but Cathy and Diane had persuaded her to wear her hair loose, and she looked younger and prettier than ever before.

They approached the altar where Mr. Wizzle, bolstered by Flynn, stood waiting. She shot him a dazzling smile and a very sweet "Stand up straight, Wizzle" before taking his arm and approaching the Justice of the Peace for the ceremony.

"Dearly beloved, we are gathered . . . "

Near the front, Boots nudged Bruno. "Hey, do you hear something? Kind of like a low humming sound?"

"Shhh," said Bruno, smiling blissfully. "This is the happiest moment of my life."

In the front row Miss Scrimmage bawled uncontrollably into a scented lace hanky. Mrs. Sturgeon held her hand and dabbed at her own eyes with a tissue. Mr. Sturgeon sat at the edge of his chair, as though trying to disassociate himself from his wife and Miss Scrimmage. Now that he had done his part and delivered the bride, he was heartily wishing himself elsewhere. He noted with grim amusement the wide smiles of pleasure on the faces of the almost one thousand students.

Pete Anderson was squirming in his seat ecstatically. This was it — the end of those tests!

Beside him, Mark beamed with happiness. Soon he'd have his newspaper back. And the Lines Department could be disbanded.

Next, Sidney. When Wizzle and Peabody were gone, maybe everyone would forget about his little accident in Miss Scrimmage's gym.

Elmer was pleased. As soon as Wizzle left, he would begin experiments in biology, chemistry, nuclear physics, mineralogy, mechanics and cryogenics. And yes, he'd focus his telescope and chart the positions of Io, second moon of Jupiter! There were great days ahead!

Chris Talbot was daydreaming along the same lines. Soon he'd have his art supplies back!

Wilbur was basking in twin blessings. He could be Hackenschleimer again, and he could re-stock the food supplies in his room. Yes, there was a big shopping trip in the near future. How long had it been since he'd last tasted peanut butter?

Cathy and Diane gripped hands and watched the service raptly. Cathy did not intend to breathe again until Wizzle and Peabody were officially pronounced man and wife. Then and only then would she believe this miracle could be happening!

Boots was looking at Bruno rather than the wedding. Oblivious of everything but the drama at the altar, Bruno sat on the edge of his chair, his face glowing pink with pleasure. Oh, well, thought Boots, he was entitled. After all, this was Bruno's wedding more than it was anybody else's. Idly, he wondered again what that low humming sound might be.

After the bridal couple had exchanged vows, the Justice of the Peace announced, "If there is any man present who can state just cause why these two people should not be joined in matrimony, let him speak now or forever hold his peace."

The silence that followed was broken by a clatter as several shingles toppled from the roof of the guest cottage. The Justice of the Peace wheeled, frowned at the falling shingles and turned back to the bride and groom. "I now pronounce you man and wife."

A great sigh rose from the spectators.

Crack! Everyone turned and stared. The front window of the guest cottage had smashed into a million pieces.

Crack! Crack! Another window shattered, too, and shingles began toppling from the roof in all directions. A low roar wafted over the crowd. Everyone gasped as the chimney seemed to disintegrate in slow motion. The bricks crumbled, bounced off the roof and rained to the ground in a series of dull thuds.

"It's the Great Lakes–St. Lawrence Lowlands fault line!" bellowed Mr. Wizzle. "Run!" He grabbed his bride and tried to lead her away from the scene. But she was not to be moved and gazed at the house in puzzled fascination.

All eyes were on the cottage, watching the woodframe walls. They almost seemed to move with the low vibrating sound.

Mr. Sturgeon jumped to his feet. The shingles were raining down in a steady stream.

There was a mighty bang as the front door, frame and all, burst from the house and shot forward.

"Heads up!" bellowed the bride. She picked up her new husband by the lapels of his coat and moved him out of harm's way. The mangled door and frame crashed to rest right where he had been standing.

A hush fell as everyone stared at the damaged cottage. The door had left a gaping hole of splintered wood. The hall chair and table had been thrown out onto the front step where they lay broken. A smashed vase spilled out water and battered carnations.

A faint hissing sound reached Boots's sensitive ears. Now, what would — He clutched at his heart. Oh no! It couldn't be . . .

The hissing grew louder, and a rapidly inflating mass of vinyl billowed from the wreckage and hovered in the air above the crowd as it filled. It obscured the sun and cast an immense shadow on the lawn as it took shape — an enormous ten-metre balloon with the unmistakable features of Walter C. Wizzle. His glasses were exaggerated, he looked pudgier than in real life, and he wore a huge black tie. On his white shirt was a red W.

Miss Peabody laughed delightedly. "Look, Wizzle! It's you!"

Boots's head sank deeper into his collar.

There were *oohs* and *aahs* as the balloon filled out completely and continued to grow to incredible size.

BOOM!!!

Tiny shreds of vinyl showered down on the shocked

spectators, many of whom were crouched beneath their chairs. People held their ears as echoes of the tremendous blast died away. A horrible silence fell, broken only by the sound of two last shingles hitting the ground.

Bruno looked around him, then stood up and cupped his hands to his mouth.

"You may kiss the bride!"

Miss Peabody swept her shocked husband off his feet and hopped daintily over the threshold of the cottage, which lay on the ground in front of them. She kissed him soundly.

The cheers were deafening.

When the wedding buffet had finished, Bruno Walton and Cathy Burton walked up to the newlyweds.

"All right, attention, everybody," called Bruno. Silence fell. "On behalf of the students of Macdonald Hall and Miss Scrimmage's, I am pleased to present our bride and groom with this gift, along with our most sincere good wishes."

There were cheers as Cathy handed Miss Peabody a large envelope. "Two tickets to Hong Kong!" she bellowed to the cheering students.

"We're touched, Burton," replied Miss Peabody. She nudged her husband. "Right, Wizzle?"

"Right."

Mr. Sturgeon leaned over to Boots. "Why Hong Kong?"

Boots shrugged nervously. "It was as far away as we could afford to send them."

Chapter 17

crystal clear

Comfortably clad in khakis and T-shirts, Bruno and Boots walked across the campus towards the Faculty Building in answer to a summons to Mr. Sturgeon's office.

"Well, Wizzle's gone, and I don't feel any different," said Boots, his voice full of anxiety. "I was scared The Fish was going to kill us before, and I'm still scared of the same thing."

"Don't worry," said Bruno calmly. "We haven't done anything lately."

"Oh, really? I suppose you didn't notice that the guest cottage lost a door, two windows, a chimney and a lot of shingles during the wedding! Remember? And that there was this big balloon that almost killed everybody!"

"Oh, that. That was three days ago. I mean, we haven't done anything *recently*." Nothing could spoil Bruno's good mood. He had just relegated his jackets and ties to the very back of his closet.

"Well," said Boots nervously, "I think The Fish was just waiting for things to get back to normal before he nailed us. We might get away with the balloon because Wizzle thought it was some kind of tribute, but we'll never get away with demolishing the house. And if The Fish found out that it was us who got Wizzle and Peabody married, we're dead!"

Bruno smiled serenely.

The two ran up the steps into the Faculty Building and presented themselves at Mr. Sturgeon's office.

"Ah, Walton and O'Neal," said the Headmaster, ushering them in and sitting them down on the bench. "I've been meaning to get to you since the wedding. It's just that things have been so hectic around here, what with the construction crews and so on."

Bruno waited patiently and Boots squirmed.

"No doubt it is you two who are behind The Coalition."

Both boys looked up in surprise.

"Oh, yes, I've heard of The Coalition. Word gets around. Now I want to hear about it from you."

"Well, sir," began Bruno, "a group of us got together and — "

"Stop," ordered the Headmaster. "The Coalition is The Committee, is it not?"

"Oh, no, sir," said Bruno. "The Coalition is an association with Miss Scrimmage's school."

"Yes," persisted Mr. Sturgeon, "but if we leave out Miss

Scrimmage's students, we are left with The Committee, are we not?"

Bruno studied the floor. "I guess so, sir."

"Excellent. Now that all our terms are properly defined, I can tell you the real reason why I called you here. I would like to acquaint you with a new regulation which I have just drafted for entry into the Macdonald Hall rule book and which I feel covers all bases. It reads as follows: *Regulations prohibit the forming by students of committees, coalitions, associations, unions, organizations, clubs, syndicates, conferences, brotherhoods, interest groups, lobbies, societies, commissions and task forces, or any other group activity of this nature, without strict supervision and approval by staff.*" He looked up and glared at them. "There will be no exceptions. I can assure you that this will be the most strictly enforced rule at Macdonald Hall. Is that clear?"

"Yes, sir."

"No, I mean is that absolutely, positively, perfectly, one hundred percent *crystal* clear?" The Headmaster was on his feet now, leaning over his desk at them.

"Yes, sir."

"Very well." A nagging doubt assailed Mr. Sturgeon's mind as he had a vision of Bruno's glowing face at the wedding. Should he demand to know if The Coalition had somehow arranged the marriage of Mr. Wizzle and Miss Peabody? No, that was an absurd question that would only serve to make him look foolish. Young boys simply could not shape people's futures like that.

And yet, when he stopped to think about it, Mr. Sturgeon could clearly recall once confidently telling himself that young boys could never cause an earthquake. The construction crew had found a device in the basement of the guest cottage which seemed to prove that earlier assumption wrong. The Committee? Who else? And if The Committee could move the earth, a simple marriage should be no problem . . .

"One more thing, boys. The indisputable success of your Committee has inspired me to form a little group of my own. I think I'll call it The Reconstruction Fund Drive. Its purpose is to raise the money to pay for repairs to our guest cottage. And since you two have so much valuable experience in these organizational matters, I am appointing you president and vice-president respectively. Volunteer dishwashing until April should cover all bills the school will incur."

"But, sir — " Bruno protested.

"That will do. I don't think we need to discuss any more particulars in this case — such as the very interesting machine that was found in the basement of the guest cottage. Let us just say that I doubt you'll have much trouble recruiting personnel. Perhaps members of the late Committee, eager to expiate their guilt . . . "

Bruno and Boots exchanged agonized glances. Dishes until April!

A smile of triumph almost made its way to the surface of Mr. Sturgeon's calm. The Committee might well be the most awesome force since the neutron bomb, but *he* was still Headmaster.

*Be sure to read the next
hilarious Macdonald Hall
adventure:*

beware the fish

much ado about spinach

Few people would argue that Macdonald Hall, located east of Toronto just off Highway 48, is not the best boarding school for boys in Canada. Even the most severe critics of modern education point to the ivy-covered walls of the Hall as a symbol of the happy blend of tradition, enlightened administration and progressive educational policies that have resulted in a rare combination of pleased parents and contented students.

Why, then, are rumblings echoing from the dining hall?

* * *

"Yes! Okay! So we need another vegetable! But why spinach?" exclaimed Boots O'Neal in disgust.

"Stewed green leaves," agreed Bruno Walton, pushing the spinach as far from the rest of his dinner as he could without actually toppling it off his plate onto the tray. "Last week they started serving raisins and figs instead of cake and ice cream. Now it's spinach instead of french fries. If this keeps up I'll be the healthiest person ever to starve to death at this school. Yeccch!"

The other boys at the dining hall table murmured their agreement.

"I told you before," said Larry Wilson, the Headmaster's office messenger, "it's the dietician. I heard Mr. Sturgeon tell her to cut costs but keep the nutrition the same."

"They're trying to kill us all!" moaned big Wilbur Hackenschleimer, who was used to having triple helpings of everything.

"You cannot possibly die," put in studious Elmer Drimsdale, "on this diet. It is nutritionally and chemically balanced." He methodically deposited some spinach into his mouth.

"You can die if you don't eat it," retorted Bruno. "We're starving! This isn't *food!*"

"Seems to me Macdonald Hall is doing a lot of cost-cutting lately," complained Boots. "Yesterday someone kicked the soccer ball out onto the highway and it got run over by a truck. End of ball, end of game. Can you imagine a school this size owning only one soccer ball?"

"And they've stopped our evening snack," added Wilbur miserably.

"I never considered it," said Elmer thoughtfully, "but the science laboratory is very low on materials and they're not being replenished. The big microscope has been broken for a week, but Mr. Hubert has made no move to have it repaired."

"No cereal at bedtime," mourned Wilbur.

"The office is crazy for saving paper," added Larry. "And

Mr. Sturgeon is using straight pins instead of paper clips and staples."

"At least The Fish gets to eat food," said Wilbur sadly. "I'll bet Mrs. Sturgeon doesn't cook garbage like this for him."

"And the thermostats are nailed at twenty in the dormitories," Boots pointed out. "Bruno and I almost froze to death last night."

"The food used to be so good here," Wilbur reminisced.

Suddenly Bruno pounded his fist onto the table. The others jumped and turned their eyes towards him. "Something's wrong," he declared. "The Hall was never like this before. The Fish always used to stand up for us and get us the things we needed. Why isn't he doing it now?"

Nobody answered.

"Larry," Bruno went on, a determined gleam in his eyes, "when you're on duty around the office, keep on the lookout. If we can find out why this is happening, we can do something about it."

"You've got it," agreed Larry. "I'll try."

* * *

"Mildred," Mr. Sturgeon, Headmaster of Macdonald Hall, announced to his wife, "I see no alternative. I am going to resign."

"Now, William," she said soothingly, "what good would that do?"

"The situation has become intolerable!" he exclaimed, pacing the small living room of the Headmaster's residence. "The budget is constantly being cut. My students are being deprived — not just of treats and luxuries, but of necessary school supplies as well. I cannot sit by and watch this going on, yet I can't do anything about it. My only course is resignation."

"That's the easy way out," his wife accused him. "You'd be abandoning our boys if you just quit. Why can't you stay on and fight?"

Mr. Sturgeon stopped pacing and eased himself into the rocking chair by the window. "I'd love to fight," he replied, "but I have nothing to fight with. The trustees do — enrolment is down and costs are soaring. They're not giving me enough money to run Macdonald Hall properly. The fact is, Mildred, if this keeps up we're going to lose the school."

"Oh, dear! Can it be that bad?"

He nodded emphatically. "At the last Board meeting there was some serious talk of putting the land and buildings up for sale."

"But this has been our home for eighteen years!"

The Headmaster shrugged unhappily. "What can I do?" He sighed. "But you do have a point: The captain should go down with the ship. I'll stay on."

* * *

Friday evening, just before midnight, the silence of the moonlit campus was disturbed by the squeaking of the window of room 306 in Dormitory 3. Bruno Walton and Boots O'Neal scrambled over the sill and jumped to the ground. They darted across the tree-lined campus, crossed the highway and nimbly scaled the wrought-iron fence around Miss Scrimmage's Finishing School for Young Ladies.

"It's a good thing we've got this place handy," said Bruno in an undertone. "If Cathy and Diane weren't feeding us we'd starve to death!" He picked up a handful of pebbles and tossed them at a second-storey window.

Cathy Burton's dark head appeared over the sill. "Your provisions will be right down," she called softly.

A few moments later a large paper bag came sailing out the window and landed at their feet. Printed on the bag in green was the message: *Happy eating. Courtesy of Miss Scrimmage's Finishing School for Young Ladies, Cathy Burton and Diane Grant, Caterers.*

Boots looked up at the open window. "You've just saved a couple of lives," he called.

"Our pleasure," answered Cathy. "Any time. Just don't expect frequent flyer miles." She waved, then shut the window.

The boys grabbed the food parcel and retraced their steps to the Macdonald Hall campus and their own Dormitory 3. They climbed back into their room.

Boots shut the window as, still in the dark, Bruno hurled himself onto his bed. There was a wild, terrified scream. Squinting in the moonlight, Boots could just make out the figure of his roommate struggling on the floor with an unknown assailant. Without hesitation he threw himself into the battle. Arms and legs thrashed. Muffled grunts filled the room. Boots could feel the intruder slowly forcing him into a headlock. He reached out blindly, grabbed a foot and started twisting.

There was a sudden click and the light came on. The arm around Boots's neck was Bruno's; the hand twisting Bruno's foot was Boots's. Standing by the light switch, pale and shaking, was Larry Wilson.

"Douse that light!" Bruno gasped angrily. "Do you want

211

The Fish on our necks?"

Larry switched off the overhead light. "Sorry," he said, still stunned.

"What the heck are you doing in our room?" demanded Boots as he and Bruno disentangled themselves and stood up.

"You asked me to keep my ears open," Larry complained. "I came here to report, not to get beaten up. You guys were out, so I lay down to wait for you. I guess I fell asleep. Do you think the racket woke up the Housemaster?"

Boots laughed. "Wake up Mr. Fudge? Don't you know about him?"

"Old Fudgie wouldn't wake up if an express train passed under his bed," said Bruno. "The first year we were here at the Hall, Boots and I came back from Scrimmage's one night and climbed into his room by mistake. If that kind of laughing in his ear won't wake him up, nothing will."

"You said you heard something," Boots reminded their visitor. "What's up?"

"You aren't going to like this very much," Larry said nervously.

"Oh, no," groaned Bruno. "I suppose they've eliminated lunch."

"Worse than that," said Larry. "The Fish has given orders to close up Dormitory 3."

There was a long moment of stunned silence.

Bruno was the first to find his voice. "No," he said quietly. "They can't do that. This is our home."

"It's being done," said Larry. "Tomorrow the orders will go out telling you where to move."

"We won't go!" stormed Boots. "We'll barricade ourselves in and hold out to the end!"

"Why?" cried Bruno. "Why would The Fish do this to us? Why?"

"Well," said Larry, "no one has actually said it, but it looks to me as if Macdonald Hall is going broke. They can't afford to run three dorms any more."

"Then let them close 1! Or 2!" howled Bruno. "But not ours! It's not fair!"

"What if you get sent to one room and me to another?" put in Boots in a strangled voice.

"No, no," soothed Larry. "You two guys are both being sent to 201."

There was another shocked silence.

"Elmer Drimsdale!" Bruno and Boots howled in unison.

"I can't live with Elmer Drimsdale!" cried Boots. "He's crazy!"

"Oh, no!" moaned Bruno, who had once been Elmer's roommate. "No, no, *no!*"

"But you guys are friends of Elmer's," Larry said, mystified.

"Yes, but that's a lot different from *living* with him!" Bruno exclaimed. "Elmer keeps ants! And fish in the bathtub! And plants all over the place! And he's always performing some experiment that takes up half the room! And he gets up at six in the morning!"

"What have we done to deserve this?" asked Boots in despair.

Bruno felt around in the dark, located the bag from Cathy and Diane and ripped it open. "Let's eat," he suggested glumly. "I always suffer better on a full stomach."

The three boys began to eat the assortment of cookies, fruit and cheese filched for them by Miss Scrimmage's girls.

"I'm getting sent to Dormitory 2 as well," Larry told them as he savoured the almost forgotten taste of a chocolate chip cookie. "I'll be across the hall in 204."

"204!" Bruno laughed despite his unhappiness. "That's Sidney Rampulsky. Be sure you pay up your accident insurance. That guy could trip over a moonbeam."

"At least he doesn't keep ants," moaned Boots.

"You know," said Bruno thoughtfully, "we're losing sight of the most important thing in this whole mess. If Macdonald Hall really is going broke, then we won't only be out of a dormitory. We'll be out of a school!"

"We're going broke, all right," said Larry. "Today I took a phone call from a real-estate company. Maybe the Hall is being put up for sale."

In the darkness of room 306, Bruno Walton's face took on a look of grim determination. "That does it!" he exclaimed. "They're starving us, they're forcing us out of our dorm, and now they're selling our school right out from under us! We won't let this happen!"

Boots, who had long ago learned to recognize the beginning of one of Bruno's crusades, felt a twinge of uneasiness. "This is all management and high finance," he protested. "It's even above The Fish. What can *we* do about it?"

"Well, I know what we *can't* do," replied Bruno. "We can't just sit back and let the Hall go down the drain! And that's exactly why the Macdonald Hall Preservation Society is meeting tomorrow at lunch!"

about the author

It has been twenty-five years since the publication of Gordon Korman's first Macdonald Hall novel, written when he was only twelve. He went on to write five more books before he even finished high school.

He now has more than fifty books to his credit, including six more Macdonald Hall titles, and, most recently, *Maxx Comedy, Jake Reinvented* and the *Dive* trilogy. He lives with his family in Long Island, New York, where he looks forward to his second quarter-century of writing for kids.